DAD BOD
DOMS
Henry

RAISA GREYWOOD

Ebook edition: 978-1-952596-01-8
Print edition: 978-1-952596-02-5

Editor: Amy Briggs
Cover Design: Eris Adderly
Photographer: FuriousFotog / Golden Czermak
Model: Kevin R. Davis
Formatting: Cynthia Starrett

TABLE OF CONTENTS

ACKNOWLEDGEMENTS

Special thanks go out to Golden Angel for coming up with such an amazing fun idea to write. I'd also like to thank Shane Starrett and Maren Smith for joining the party, along with Addison Cain for loaning us Shane's soul for a few months. Without them, the Dad Bod Doms wouldn't be a thing.

I also want to thank Martine M. for her insights into mental health, AJ Renard for helping me understand the fluidity of a power-exchange relatinship, and EJ Frost for her assistance with the mysteries of criminal law.

As always, Engineer Hubby, Mr. Greywood, deserves the outest of shouts for his unwavering support and faith in me, and for being my own beloved Dad Bod Dom. Love you to the moon and back baby.

Want to see what I'm up to next? Join my Raunchy Renegades at [http://www.facebook.com/groups/272762356598383/]. You can also sign up for my Newsletter [https://www.subscribepage.com/dad_bods]. As a bonus, everyone who signs up will recieve a FREE exclusive short story following up with Henry and Natalie.

When four old friends arrive for their annual camping trip stressed out and defeated, they discover each of them is going through a rough patch in his relationship and his life.

Unwilling to give in to the inevitable, they decide to make a pact: by next year's camping trip, they'll have reclaimed their confidence and their submissives.

Desperate times call for Dad Bod Doms.

PROLOGUE

Henry

"The Dad Bod Doms," we chorused, doing a male fist bump thing as we prepared to leave for our respective homes after our yearly camping trip. Our cars were packed, and I was itching to get on the road.

It was a pact. An agreement between four old friends. Maybe more a challenge to recapture the lost spark that used to make our marriages so successful. At least Ray, Faris, and Logan were talking to their wives. After years of failed fertility treatments and demanding careers, my relationship with Natalie needed some help.

Whole days went by without a word from either of us. We didn't fight—at least not like what appeared to be happening between Faris and Leyla—but things weren't right and the distance between us was almost painful.

Although I thought it was stupid at first, the more I considered the idea, the better I liked it. Instead of stopping for the night halfway through the sixteen-hour trip back to Minneapolis, I drove straight home. I couldn't wait to start making things right with Natalie.

By the time I pulled into our driveway, I was so tired I could barely see straight and didn't bother unpacking my car. After taking a shower in the guest bathroom, I crept into our bedroom. Natalie was already asleep, which was no great surprise. She never stayed up much past ten, and it was already almost two in the morning.

Sprawled on her stomach with the sheet kicked away, she looked like an angel. Her pale skin shimmered in the moonlight, gleaming like alabaster. The ceiling fan whirring lazily overhead stirred a few strands of her silvery hair and I resisted the urge to brush it away to reveal the curve of her shoulder.

There was no time like the present to get started on the Dad Bod Dom Challenge. It had been awhile since we'd last made love. Actually, it had been close to a year because I was an idiot. My dissatisfaction with my job shouldn't have spilled over into our relationship.

What I wouldn't give for a do-over. I'd have never let us drift so far apart. Between our respective jobs and the heartbreak of realizing we'd never have a child together, I'd let our marriage flounder. No more. I was the dominant in this relationship, and it was past time I acted like it.

Thankfully, I remembered how to wake a sleeping wife and make her happy about it. Settling in bed next to her, I drew the scent of her floral perfume deep into my lungs. It was criminally expensive, but I loved it.

She grunted irritably, making me smile. I kept it up, brushing soft kisses over her shoulders until she rolled over. I circled a dark peach nipple with a fingertip, remembering how she used to love having them clamped.

No. Bad Dad Bod Dom.

Tonight was for reconnecting with each other. I needed to tell her how much I loved her, and I wanted to hear her say it back. Our playroom in the basement could wait. Lowering my head, I pulled her nipple into my mouth and sucked gently, then teased the other to ripe turgidity with my fingers.

She moaned and arched her back, her head falling to the side as her hips shifted upwards. Her slim hand drifted between her legs and I let her play with herself for a few minutes before covering her fingers with mine.

Waking with a jerk, she let out a frightened squeak and tried to pull her hand free. "Henry? What—"

I kissed my way up her chest to her lips, my cock throbbing at the wetness coating my fingers. "Shh, baby girl. Just relax and let me love you."

Circling her clit with my thumb, I pressed a finger inside her and she bucked against my hand, letting out a soft whimper of pleasure. It was good for a start, but I wanted to give her more. I kissed her again, relishing her passionate whine, then moved slowly down her body to lay between her legs.

The soft fragrance of her heated passion wafted over me as I lowered my face to her core and licked the sweetness from her swollen flesh. I missed the platinum ring she used to have in her clit hood, but she'd taken it out when we started fertility treatments. Deciding not to go there, I got back to work.

Fresh arousal coated my lips and chin as I devoured her, learning her body all over again. A finger pressed against her g-spot still made her spasm and cry out with delight. I sucked her clit into my mouth, teasing the sensitive nub with the tip of my tongue.

She pushed her pussy into my face and tangled her hands in my hair. "Henry! Oh, God, please! I need to come!"

I almost lost control and nutted right there. She

remembered. After all this time, Natalie didn't forget to ask for permission. Giving her clit one last suck, I crawled up and settled between her thighs, then positioned myself at her entrance.

"You can come with me, baby." I eased my cock into her tight channel, gritting my teeth against the urge to pound her into the mattress. "Just a little longer."

"Feels so good."

"I love you, Natalie Mercer."

Instead of answering, she kissed me, her lips hard and desperate, frantic with need. The taste of her consumed me as I reached between our straining bodies to thumb her clit. I wasn't going to last much longer, and I needed her ready. Balls aching, I slid an arm behind her thigh, opening her to my possession. Her inner walls rippled around me, heralding her orgasm.

"Come for me, baby. Let go."

Crying out, she exploded, her hips bucking wildly as she chased her pleasure. Unable to hold back, I had no choice but to follow her into bliss.

Panting softly, she let her head fall back to the pillow. Wetness glistened on her lashes, but I didn't worry. Natalie sometimes cried after climaxing. Kissing her eyelids, I brushed the tears away and rolled to my side before I crushed her.

"Hi, honey. I'm home," I murmured, nuzzling the soft skin under her ear.

"I didn't expect you until tomorrow." Her voice steadied, and she turned to let me spoon her.

"I missed you." I kissed the back of her neck. "We have a lot of catching up to do, but tomorrow after we've both had a good night's sleep."

My eyes drifted shut. After too little sleep and

monumentally good sex with the love of my life, there was no way I'd be able to stay awake. It was enough to have her in my arms again.

Natalie

Shit, shit, shit!

My pussy dripping, I eased out of Henry's arms and scuttled away as carefully as I could. Thankfully, he was out cold, his snoring a familiar nighttime melody.

Had he seen anything? The letter I'd left, or the empty closets? Grabbing a T-shirt and some jeans, I crept out and dressed in the hallway, praying he'd stay asleep. There wasn't time to clean out the last of my stuff from the spare room I used as a studio.

What the hell was wrong with me? Why hadn't I said no? And why on earth had he decided he wanted sex? He hadn't so much as spoken more than a few words at a time to me in months. I grimaced and hopped on one foot to put my sock on. I might not have been the best at communication, but at least I'd tried.

Henry hadn't changed a bit. He still knew how to make me go off like fireworks. Worse, for my libido and my ability to say no, he still had that damned Prince Albert piercing that felt so, so good sliding into me.

I'd been so stupid. I wanted one more night in the house we shared. Like a swan song for our marriage, it was supposed to be my chance to say goodbye to everything. Martine, my therapist, said it would be good for me, but neither of us expected him to come home early. I made a mental note to yell at her during our next session. She was big on personal reminders like that.

Henry didn't scare me physically. He might be a deviously imaginative sadist, but it would be anathema to him to cause me bodily harm.

But there were all kinds of hurt, and not all of them were physical.

I took one last tour of the house, making sure I hadn't forgotten anything. The door to the room Henry used as his man cave remained steadfastly closed. I never went in there, not even to clean. My feet were silent on the hardwood floor I'd once found so charming, and I wondered if Henry would sell the place once I was gone.

Maybe he'd get another sub. The thought made me unaccountably jealous and sad, and I wondered why I cared.

Moving into the kitchen, I straightened the folder containing the documents Henry would need, but my fist clenched around the house key I meant to leave behind. I forced myself to let it go, flinching at the metallic jingle when it fell to the wood surface of the dining room table Henry bought at an estate auction just before our second anniversary. The thick Queen Anne legs still had rope marks from our first play session in our new home, and…

Stop it.

My body buzzed from his lovemaking and I forced myself to focus. Grabbing my purse, I set the alarm and walked out, steadfastly keeping my gaze fixed on my car. For once, I was going to focus on me. Not on the happy house full of laughing children I'd always wanted but would never have, or on the man who, until tonight and his unprecedented intimacy, was more roommate than husband.

How had my life gone so sideways? I wished I had the nerve to confront him and tell him I was leaving. I wasn't putting the entire blame for our failed relationship on Henry. It took two people to make a marriage work. Maybe I should have been more insistent about talking, or done something else to make things better. I grimaced, remembering the last time I tried.

Knowing his work schedule was a clusterfuck, I made an appointment with my own damned husband to make sure he got home at a reasonable hour. I ordered a steak and lobster supper from what used to be our favorite restaurant, dolled myself up in a slinky dress, and...sat at the table for almost three hours while he worked late. It was the last time I asked him to do something.

A part of me still loved Henry. He was my first in so many ways. First lover, first husband...first dom. *Only dom*, I corrected myself. I willingly gave up control to him and loved every single moment. Husband, lover, sexy sadistic bastard sometimes. Henry was all those things, and at one time I'd counted him as my best friend.

Then he'd set me adrift without a lifeline, and left nothing to hold me together. To say I was terrified was a monumental fucking understatement, but I had to go. I needed to find the Natalie that used to be. The brave one who wasn't afraid to take a train across Europe, or walk up to a handsome man and ask him out. The old Natalie—because the new one sucked.

"Fake it until you make it, hooker," I muttered. When my phone connected with the dash display, I turned up Nine Inch Nails as loud as I could stand it. Henry always hated my choice of music, but he wasn't going to be around to complain anymore. Brushing away my tears, I drove away.

Fuck Henry Mercer and the horse he rode in on.

CHAPTER ONE

Henry

Rolling over, I stretched out an arm, expecting Natalie's warm body still in bed next to me. When I found nothing but cold sheets, I opened my eyes and grunted sourly. She had a standing date with an elliptical at the gym every morning at six. I respected her dedication to fitness, but I wished I'd asked her to skip it this morning.

I rubbed my flabby gut, knowing I should have gotten my ass out of bed and joined her. She used to love tracing the ridges of the six-pack I'd sported back in the day, and watching her cute ass bounce while she worked out was definitely worth waking up for.

Deciding to be productive, I got dressed and headed into the kitchen to start a pot of coffee, then swore softly, remembering it was a school day. Natalie wouldn't be home until late afternoon. Worse, I had to be at work the next day too.

Fortunately, it gave me time to clean up my camping gear. I sent her a quick text to wish her a good day at work, belatedly adding that I loved her. An answering text came back almost immediately.

Natalie: *Look on the kitchen table.*

I picked up the manilla folder, noting the key next to it. Sitting down, I opened it and my gut roiled as I read the top page.

Henry,

I'm not sure what happened last night. I don't know why you came home early, or why you wanted sex. I also don't know why I didn't say no. Maybe I just wanted to think you cared for a little while.

Aside from last night, which I think we can agree was just weird and out of character for both of us, I don't remember the last time we had sex, the last time you touched me, or had a meaningful conversation with me.

I know you hate your boss, and the only time you talk about the future is to ask me when we'll have enough saved so you can retire.

You don't know that I hated mine too, or that I died a little inside every day I went to work. If you make it home while I'm still awake, you yell, drink a few beers, complain about supper (and I admit I'm not the greatest cook), then play in that stupid game room until you pass out.

Speaking of which, I retired from teaching at the end of the last school year to follow my dreams of painting professionally. I tried to tell you, but you put on headphones and blew me off.

If your job is so bad, maybe you should find another instead of bitching about it. I realized recently that our lives don't change just because we want them to be different. We have to want them to be different badly enough to do something about it.

The banking passwords are on the attached page, along with the household bills.

If you have any questions, you can email my attorney. I'm not going to ask for alimony or any stupid shit like that. We'll split everything 60/40. You earned more, so you'll get the sixty percent and we'll each keep our own retirement accounts. The house is yours. Sell it and split the proceeds, or keep it and buy me out. There's nothing I want in it, but I'm sure we can be adult enough to behave until we get our assets separated.

Anyway, that's all I wanted to tell you.

Best wishes,

Natalie

The paper crackled as I squeezed my fist around it.

"Fuck!" I let the letter fall and rubbed my face, scowling at the divorce paperwork in the folder. "Natalie, what are you thinking?"

Jumping up, I took the stairs two at a time to our bedroom and yanked the closet door open. All her clothes were gone. Her dresser drawers were also empty, along with everything from her bathroom. Spinning on my heel, I strode down the hall to the room she used as an office slash studio. Nothing remained except the watercolor she'd done of Lake Tahoe where we'd gotten married and the faint odor of turpentine.

Natalie wasn't stupid, but damn it, she did some dumbass stuff sometimes. How the hell did she expect to support herself with a bunch of paint and canvas? Had she found another job? Where?

I went downstairs and got a beer, then drained nearly half of it in one swallow. Reaching for my phone, I tapped her contact to call her, but it went immediately to voicemail. Maybe she'd answer a text.

Me: *Come home, Natalie. I'm ready to talk now.*

Natalie: *I can't. Don't call me again, please.*

With a roar of anger, I threw the phone across the room, the impact shattering the screen. I stalked to the cupboard, and grabbed a bottle of scotch. How the fuck was I supposed to fix our relationship if she was already leaving me?

***

Dragging myself into work the following morning had one benefit. Despite the pounding in my head from a raging hangover, it kept my mind off losing Natalie. The coffee I was swilling like water, plus a handful of aspirin would cure me eventually.

"Henry, see me in my office in five minutes, please," Bethany Thompson, my boss, snapped, speed walking past my cubicle. The hem of her skirt flared around toned legs, and her heels sounded like gunshots on the tile floor. Fuck's sake, did she have to wear those damned power suits every day? She had to change whenever she went out on the production floor, costing us time we didn't always have.

"Why yes, I had a wonderful vacation, thanks for asking," I muttered, grimly sipping my cooling coffee. Taking my time, I brought up the designs I'd been working on and emptied my coffee cup before crossing the cubicle farm to Bethany's office overlooking the floor. Tapping on the door frame, I walked in, scowling when she didn't look up.

"Have a seat, please," she ordered, shuffling papers on her desk.

I settled into the uncomfortable chair. "What can I do for you?"

"I'll be asking Sara Lyons to join us shortly. We're handing over the S-79 robotics project to her. You'll be spending the next few months getting her up to speed, then we're transferring you to a team lead position on the production floor."

"Excuse me? I've spent the last two years on that project, and you're promoting a kid over me?"

Bethany looked up, her blue eyes expressionless. "Yes. I felt Sara would be the best fit for the position."

"May I ask why?"

"Sara is personable and a team player. She dresses the part, while you haven't shown up to work in anything but jeans and a T-shirt in the whole time I've worked here. She can develop a rapport with both our customer and suppliers, and frankly, she has more management potential than you do."

Natalie was right. Things didn't change because I wanted them to. Bethany's position had originally been offered to me, but I wanted to go into project management instead of administration. She apparently saw that as a threat, and never made a secret of the fact she didn't like me. I hadn't realized she'd be petty enough to yank two years of my life out from under me—the same two years I could have used to reconnect with my wife. That irritated me more than anything else.

I stood and nodded. "Okay."

"Okay?" Her brow arching, she smirked.

"Yep. Okay. May I?" I asked, reaching for a notepad on her desk.

"Sure." She pushed the pad and a pen toward me.

It took surprisingly little time to get rid of years of stress and dissatisfaction with just a few words scrawled on paper. I turned to walk out, but stopped when she spoke.

"You can't quit!" she blustered. "What is Sara supposed to do without—"

I gave her a smile that always used to work on Natalie. It was the one that said, *be quiet now before something bad happens*. Bethany's eyes widened and she pressed her lips together, her hands trembling. Huh. Maybe if I'd turned on the sadist's charm when she first started working here, I might have gotten something useful out of her instead of bullshit.

"Bethany, I don't care. I can't count the number of overtime hours I put into this project. I did everything you asked without complaint, and gave you more than you had any business expecting from a person you had no intention of rewarding. I don't give a damn what Sara does, or how far your department sinks. You said she had management potential, so now she gets to prove it. Have a nice life. I'll stop in HR on my way out."

I returned to my desk, unsurprised when a security guard joined me while I was boxing my personal belongings. Still beaming a feral smile, I packed Natalie's picture and my coffee cup, then said, "Thanks for the escort."

Whistling, I crossed the production floor, nodding at friends and coworkers. Although there were a few people I'd miss, I wasn't about to change my mind. I should have done this a long time ago.

When I reached HR, my friend George Anderson met me at the door. "I just heard," he said softly, ushering me into his office. "Are you sure about this? We have an opening in the South Carolina facility. You'd be a good fit for it, and it comes with a pretty healthy salary increase."

Although the offer was tempting, I shook my head and sat across the desk from him. "No. I'm going to take the twenty and out retirement option. That covers my insurance and pension, plus I have six weeks of accrued vacation."

George sighed and pushed a hand through his thinning hair. "That takes about a month to process."

"Use my vacation time."

"How would you feel about us moving Bethany? Quite frankly, I can find a department manager anywhere, but a good engineer is a bigger challenge.

Would you stay if we put her in another department and gave you her job?"

"No."

Thankfully, he didn't ask for my reasons. "Okay. You got it. Hell, as long as you've been here, your stock options alone will fund a very comfortable retirement. Can we at least put you on the list as a private contractor?"

"No, at least not anytime soon." I'd intended to save that stock fund for a rainy day, but I supposed it was raining hard enough now to break into it.

I signed the forms George gave me, then sat through the exit video reminding me of my benefits and the NDA I'd signed. An hour later, I walked out, feeling like an inmate released after a lifetime in prison. For a brief moment, I wondered if Natalie felt that way when she left her teaching position. I had to admit she had a point on a few things, but would it have killed her to try one last time?

To my surprise, Bethany chased me across the parking lot, breathing hard when she caught up. "You fucking loser," she hissed, her face pale with fury. "How dare you?"

Man, what I wouldn't give to strap my ex-boss to a St. Andrew's cross and practice my single-tail work. Cocking my head, I entertained the notion of taking her into my basement playroom for a lesson in manners. I wouldn't, of course. She'd probably have me arrested for assault. Worse, she might like it. I shuddered, making no effort to hide my distaste. "You're entitled to your opinion," I murmured.

The thought gave me an idea, and a smile twitched my lips upward. The playroom was intact, although it hadn't been used in years. Maybe I *should* visit a club and...*no*. I didn't want anyone else in my playroom but Natalie, and the thought of some strange sub in our space made me nauseous. That didn't mean I couldn't find some refresher courses.

Bethany flushed and snapped her mouth shut, making me wonder what she saw on my face. Still smirking, I watched her attempt to gather her composure.

"Asshole," she muttered. "Good riddance."

"Indeed." I drove away, the seeds of a plan blooming in my mind.

Natalie

"Are you sure this is going to work?" I asked, still trying to get my thoughts off Henry and focus on what I was supposed to be doing. Thankfully, he hadn't tried to call again. I felt like shit for leaving while he was asleep, but it would take another two-hour session with Martine before I could muster up the lady balls for a confrontation.

My canvases were arrayed around the gallery, a few still unframed, but in position for my first exhibit in less than two days. Although I'd been dreaming of this for most of my adult life, it made me queasy with nerves and excitement.

"Yes, darling!" Chloe Benson kissed my cheek, pulling me into a one-armed hug smelling of Chanel number five. Well into her seventies, Chloe was wealthy, connected, and had zero social filter. I wanted to be just like her when I grew up.

"I'm not sure about it though. I mean, isn't the whole Fifty Shades thing cliché?"

"Well, yes, but we're not doing that." Chloe's six-foot five body moved gracefully across the floor and she straightened an acrylic over wood of Persephone bound in rose vines on its easel.

"You're throwing a black-tie masquerade for an unsold artist," I replied, trying to hide a smile. "I think people are going to connect the dots."

"Smarty pants." Chloe patted my cheeks with white-gloved hands and peered at me over cat-eye spectacles. "Your art is rich, decadent, tasteful erotica and will command thousands. I promise. It isn't anything as pedestrian as those claptrap novels."

"Those claptrap novels made millions. Besides, isn't tasteful erotica an oxymoron?"

Chloe laughed, tossing her head back. "Maybe you won't make millions, but you won't have any trouble feeding yourself while you create the next series."

"I already started it." I moved toward the rose painting, lifting a gentle finger to trace a ridge of red paint across Persephone's belly. "Beauty in pain," I whispered.

Chloe pulled me into a hug and stroked my back. "Aw, sweetie, come here and let Uncle Charles take care of everything."

I laughed and sniffed back tears. "You're in a dress and pearls today. That means you're Chloe."

"Hush and let me play uncle for a few minutes." Giving me one last squeeze, she let me go. "I know it hurts now, but you're going to be okay. Maybe you'll meet a nice guy at your show and your next exhibit will be hot enough to make me wish I still had a dick that worked."

Laughing, I shook my head. "I haven't gotten rid of the old one yet. A new dick is the last thing I need."

Talk about fake it until you make it. Every time I thought about Henry, I wanted to curl into a ball and sob my heart out, but I'd already spent enough time doing that. After almost twenty years of marriage, it was time for big girl panties.

Chloe chuckled and took my arm, then walked me into her office. Pulling out a bottle of wine, she poured two glasses. "Here's to my newest star, Natalie Kane." She drained her glass, then added, "Now to the most important question of all."

"What's that?"

"What are you going to wear?"

I blinked and nearly dropped my glass. "Um… I—"

"Shit, girl!" Chloe pulled out a slim phone and drummed her nails on the desk while it rang. When it was answered, she said, "Ladies, we have a fashion emergency. Get everyone to my gallery now with all the size eight cocktail dresses you have. The sexier the better."

How the hell did she guess my dress size so accurately? "Wait! I have a black dress I wore to a company party once. It's fine."

"Natalie, so help me, I will turn you over my knee," Chloe warned. "You are not wearing some middle-class white chick dress to my event."

"I *am* a middle-class white chick."

"Don't worry. We won't hold it against you." Turning her attention back to her call, Chloe said, "Bring lunch from that Indian place on Fourth, and a case of champagne. We'll have an early showing of Natalie's work."

Thirty minutes later, drag queens from all over the city arrived *en masse*, bearing food, booze, and dozens of rolling racks full of sumptuous frocks. They stripped me down to my panties and made me into their own personal Barbie while getting me drunk off my ass.

I couldn't remember having so much fun. Like,

ever. I opened my mouth, accepting a bite of butter chicken from Tyler. No, Tallulah. No, Tyler. He wasn't dressed.

"Let's try this one," Chloe said, holding up a black river of lacy fabric. "I'm thinking it's a definite maybe."

I held up my arms obediently, allowing Chloe to slip the dress over my head, then closed my eyes and let my worries go. They'd make me gorgeous, no matter what I wore, and I was drunk enough not to care what it took.

"Damn, girl. I think I'm gonna turn straight."

The crowd went silent, then burst into uproarious laughter. I opened my eyes and stared into the portable three-way mirror. I hadn't worn anything so revealing since the last time Henry took me to a club, but I loved it immediately.

Made of sheer black lace embroidered with flowers, the bodice split to my navel, revealing a pale swath of skin before falling to my ankles. Boning in the sides pushed my ample breasts up into luxurious cleavage. My pink panties showed through, incongruous with the decadent fabric.

"Fuck me sideways. I need so much Spanx, but yes to the dress!"

"No Spanx, little girl. You need a Brazilian and a black thong," Tyler replied.

"And shoes. Sexy, kinky shoes," Chloe added.

I heard one grumble above the noise of approval. Turning, I looked at Eric. Standing with his arms crossed, he scowled at me. "I hate how you look better in that than I do," he muttered.

I rushed to him, my bare feet slipping on the tile. "Except I can't make it nearly as fabulous as you can."

"Brat." He gave me a smile and a brief hug, then handed me a glass of champagne.

Knowing I needed to cut myself off, and maybe eat more than a few bites of food, I sipped slowly. "Thanks, you guys… I… Thanks."

"Oh, my mascara," Chloe moaned, waving at her eyes. "Somebody slap her ass and make her smile."

Eric obliged, popping my butt hard enough to sting, but it broke the tension. I dredged up a smile, trying not to remember the last time Henry spanked me.

This was my new normal. I had wonderful friends and a bright future doing something I loved. My personal modified serenity prayer came to mind.

"God grant me the serenity to tell everything I can't change to fuck right off," I announced, holding my glass high to the cheers of my fans.

CHAPTER TWO

Henry

Feeling freer than I had in a long time, I stopped to grab something to eat and a fresh bottle of scotch as a reward for myself. I might not have my wife, but today was going to be a goddamned celebration. At least for part of it. I also bought a new phone, along with a case durable enough to be thrown against a wall, then drove home.

Pushing the papers aside, I sat down at the kitchen table and devoured the breakfast burrito, washing it down with a few swallows from the bottle of scotch. Given what Natalie said in her note, I wondered how she might have reacted to what I'd done. Hell, she might have celebrated with me, but I didn't fool myself into thinking it would solve our relationship woes.

The first problem would be finding her. I pulled up Ray's contact, but my finger hovered over the touchscreen. Did I really want to air my dirty laundry to my friends? No, but if I wanted to find Natalie, I needed help. Gritting my teeth, I hit the call icon, then waited until it rang through.

"Hey, dude!" Ray said. "How are things going?"

"It's going great. Natalie and I are just starting to work on pulling our relationship back together," I lied smoothly. "Got a question. Do you still have contacts in the service? I need to find the location of a cell phone. Natalie lost hers, and we haven't been able to find it."

"Sorry to hear that. Could she just pull her stuff off the cloud and buy a new one?"

"I asked, but she says she saved everything to her SD card and we never got one of those tracking apps." I paused a moment, knowing I was asking one of my closest friends to do something illegal. "I just hate to disappoint her when we're trying to get things back on track, you know?"

"Yeah, I get it. I'll make some calls and let you know what I find out. Oh, while I have you on the phone, congratulate Natalie for her gallery show. Ally saw it on Facebook the other day, but we won't be able to make it. You must be incredibly proud of her."

I tightened my hand around the bottle of scotch, my fury welling. A fucking gallery show? The last thing I remembered seeing of hers was that watercolor landscape. It was pretty, but I could buy shit just like it in discount store poster bins. Did Natalie understand how hard it could be for an artist to make a living? She wasn't one to make snap decisions like that, and I didn't understand what she could have been thinking. Hell, I didn't know art from my ass. Maybe I was wrong, but I was worried sick on top of being furious with her.

"Still there, buddy?"

"Yeah, sorry. I guess I walked through a dead spot. I'll give her the message, and thanks for the help finding her phone."

Ending the call, I went upstairs to the game room, still holding the bottle. I brought up a browser on my computer, then typed her name into the search bar. Nothing came up, except her social media profiles. Although I'd never seen much point in it, I made an account on Facebook, hoping to figure out where she'd gone. Unfortunately, her profile was locked, and I doubted she'd accept a friend request from me.

There wasn't anything about an art show though. On a whim, I tried her maiden name and hit paydirt with the local newspaper and a gallery website.

"Best new artist of the year, huh?" I muttered to myself, ordering the laughably overpriced ticket to the black-tie masquerade party about forty-five minutes away. Stupid gimmicks. But if going to that gallery was what it took to get my wife back, I'd put on a goddamned tux and do it.

First, I needed to make some plans, and I had less than four days to do it. By the end of the week, Natalie would be a very sorry little girl.

After shooting Ray a quick text to call him off, I threw open the basement door and scowled at the musty smell. Turning the lights on, I stomped down the stairs. Everything was just as we'd left it, but covered in a thick coating of dust. Swearing under my breath, I started cleaning up.

Two hours later, the basement was as good as it was going to get, which was certainly good enough for Natalie. Belatedly, I wished I'd left it the way it was. Having her clean the playroom naked on her hands and knees after I beat her ass would have been entertaining. Smirking, I started a list of all the fun things I could do to my wife, adding the chore to the top.

As an afterthought, I mounted a digital video camera on a tripod facing the play area, sending the feed to my computer. I wasn't about to share the footage of Natalie's come to Jesus moments, but it might be useful.

After hurrying through another shower, I

considered stopping at the bank to have her name removed from our accounts, but decided against it. I'd have her home and kneeling at my feet soon enough. Instead, I drove to the mall and got fitted for a tuxedo, then detoured to the hair place. When the stylist finished, I blinked at my reflection.

Maybe Bethany had a point about my appearance. The unkempt gray beard hadn't done me any favors, and the new haircut took years off my face. Instead of looking like Jerry Garcia on a bender, I looked… Well, not like an aging rock star after a three-day drunk-fest. If I still had abs, I might even be able to pass for a model on one of Natalie's romance novels.

It didn't mean I'd be showing up to work in a suit anytime soon. Hell, I wasn't going to be showing up to work at all. Grinning, I paid my bill, giving the stylist a generous tip, then stopped for supper before going home to plot. I still had to go to the supermarket too. Once I had her, I had no intention of leaving the house until she agreed to stay where she belonged.

The thought raised a very important question. How was I going to get Natalie home without getting arrested? Ray or Faris might have some ideas, but I wasn't about to involve them, nor could I exactly ask Google how to kidnap my wife.

Shit. Maybe I'd just wing it and see what happened. My biggest problem was that I couldn't think of anything I might have left to use for blackmail, aside from our shared bank accounts. Her lawyer would have that straightened out in no time.

I finally fell asleep, visions of dragon tongues and butt plugs coated with warming lube dancing in my head. Merry fucking Christmas and ho ho ho.

***

The house was as secure as I could make it, including plywood nailed over the basement windows, plus a brand-new deadbolt on the door. The downstairs bathroom was stocked with towels and personal care products. The basement refrigerator was filled with prepackaged food, and I even set up a spare coffee pot along with a microwave. We were going to stay down there until Natalie came to her senses.

Best of all, everything I planned would be on Natalie's list of favorite things. Chase, capture, confinement, struggle-fucking. She loved it all.

Thankfully, my rush order of all sorts of wicked e-stim toys arrived just in time for the fun. I'd never tried electroshock with her, and there was no time like the present for the experiment.

I straightened the bow tie on my rented tux, cocking my head at my reflection. I didn't look too bad for an old dude, and the mask made me unrecognizable.

I'd eventually tell her who I was, but not right away. She needed to pay for her mistakes first. To that end, I packed a makeshift kidnapping kit in a small laptop bag, including duct tape, a voice synthesizer I used for a Halloween costume once, and an unopened bag of zip ties. As an afterthought, I tossed in a bondage hood Natalie had hated. It locked around her neck and covered her face completely aside from an opening for her nose and a zipper over her mouth.

When my Uber dropped me at the gallery, I blinked at the line of people standing outside. Other people dressed in formalwear bypassed the line, entering between velvet ropes guarded by two men in black suits. I hoped the ferociously expensive ticket would gain me entrance that way. If not, I'd burn that bridge later.

"May I see your ticket, sir?" one of the guards asked, holding out his hand.

I fished the sheet of paper from my coat pocket and handed it over.

"Thank you, sir. Enjoy the exhibit."

"Thanks." At the guard's pointed nod, I put on the mask and made my way inside. It was crowded, but not as badly as I expected it to be, judging by the line outside the door. Playing softly in a corner, a string quartet provided background music, adding elegance to the event. A server walked by and offered me champagne.

Taking a glass, I scanned the room for Natalie, but couldn't find her. Grumbling under my breath, I decided to see what all the fuss was about and actually look at her work.

Angry slashes of red and black covered the first canvas, the paint thick enough to appear almost three-dimensional. It was a nude cradling an empty blanket, silvery shards of ice binding her throat and wrists. Stark and visceral, it took my breath away. A discreet blue tag on the frame marked it sold, and I blinked in shock at the price.

What happened to the Natalie I remembered who painted watercolor landscapes? Judging by the number of canvases, all bearing blue tags, she'd been gone for some time. I walked to the last one, swallowing hard at the woman entwined in thorny vines, blood red paint seeming to trickle from wounds. Next to her, a shadowy male figure held out a surprisingly realistic pomegranate.

They must have been Hades and Persephone, and the one bound in ice was Demeter.

"Natalie is very talented, isn't she," a man said, gliding up to stand next to me. He was several inches taller than me and seemed almost ageless in his thirties-era tuxedo.

"Yes, she is," I murmured.

"I'm sorry all her sale pieces are gone, but we'll show her again next year. She's already planning another series."

"I'm afraid they're out of my budget, but they're very compelling."

"Have you had a chance to meet her? She's in the corner next to Aphrodite. This is the *Bound Goddess* series." Pointing at the woman bound in ice, he added, "I'm particularly fond of Demeter over there."

Surrounded by people, Natalie laughed and lifted her glass. What the fuck was she wearing? I wouldn't have taken her to a club dressed like that, and she was out in public? God, she was gorgeous. Her lacy black dress concealed nothing, yet seemed to hide everything important. It was like a red flag to a bull, and I resisted the urge to cover her with my jacket.

Her silvery hair had streaks of blue and purple, and was twisted into a complicated spiral decorated with feathers. Dark shadow highlighted her eyes, the paint drawn to resemble a harlequin mask. Vivid red lips pursed into a bowed smile as she chatted with her fans. Sultry and seductive in that sinful dress, I'd never seen Natalie look more beautiful.

"No, I'm afraid I haven't."

Holding out a hand, the man said, "Charles Benson."

Accepting the offered handshake, I said, "A pleasure to meet you. Are you the owner of the gallery?"

"Yes," Charles pulled a business card from a

holder. "Call me tomorrow and we'll put you on the mailing list for Natalie's next show."

"Thanks. How did you discover her?"

Charles directed a warm smile toward her. "She came to one of my shows about six months ago asking if I'd take a few of her paintings on consignment. The rest is history." He inclined his head, then turned. "I have to mingle, but please avail yourself of the buffet and enjoy the gallery."

I moved closer to Natalie, but stayed in the background. She was engaged in conversation with a tall, bald man and a tiny woman with black spiky hair. The woman pulled her into a hug, squealing gleefully. Letting out a soft laugh, the man gently pried her away from Natalie and turned slightly, a grin tugging at the edges of a very familiar scar.

Holy fuck. I didn't know the woman, but that was Patrick Murphy from Stronghold. I touched my mask to make sure it was in place. Him recognizing me was the last thing I needed.

"Thank you for letting us have the whole collection," the woman said. "It's going to be perfect for the dungeon."

"No, Lexie. These are going to Marquis," Patrick replied. "Stronghold already has art above the bar."

I'd met Ray, Faris, and Logan at Stronghold years ago. Hell, they'd hooked up with their wives there, and Natalie and I had made several trips to visit. On one memorable weeklong vacation, all four of us had even taken our wives to The Castle in Ohio.

The Castle wasn't just a club. It was a complete immersion into kink located in a real castle brought over stone by stone from Europe. I had to smile at the memory. Natalie first admitted to being a masochist in the dungeon while under the care of their whip master.

I was a relative newbie back then, but the things he could do with that single-tail pushed me into learning everything I could about impact play just to please her.

"Good idea. We should invite Natalie to DC and let her do the installation."

"If I'd realized you two were the buyers, I'd have given you mate's rates," Natalie said, grinning at them. "You might like my next series better for a dungeon though. It's going to be called *Beauty in Pain*, and will include actual bondage furniture."

Patrick handed her a business card, then wrapped a thick arm around his woman. "I'd like to discuss commissioning a few pieces. My accountant is going to have a coronary if I buy another collection, but I'm very interested in what you're planning."

Natalie beamed and typed her number into the phone Patrick handed her. Leaving them to their conversation, I grunted and went to the buffet, blinking at the massive bowl of iced caviar surrounded by crackers and toast points. Cutting off her finances wasn't going to get me what I wanted, not when she'd surpassed six months' worth of my earnings in one evening. I couldn't decide whether to be jealous or so proud I could burst. It was a sickening mixture of both. Against the odds, she'd made her life's dream into a marketable success.

"Thank you for coming to see my work. I'm the artist, Natalie Kane."

My cock twitched at the sound of Natalie's soft, husky voice and I spun around, nearly dropping the plate I'd loaded with lobster-filled puff pastry. "A pleasure," I replied, deepening my voice in hopes of disguising it. "Your work is amazing."

She gave me a brilliant grin and flushed pink. "Thanks. I really appreciate you saying that. Please, enjoy the party, and let me know if you have any questions."

"Where did you get your inspiration?" I asked. I should have let her go before she recognized me, but the question came out. Had I ever known her? The woman standing next to me wasn't the Natalie I remembered. Yet maybe she was. She used to be bold, brazen, utterly charming, and without social filter. Twenty years ago, she wouldn't have batted an eye at the scandalous concoction of lace she was wearing.

Her smile faded, leaving a pensive expression on her pretty face. "Life experience, I suppose. Artists often portray their emotions, and I guess you could say the same about me." The grin returned, although it didn't reach her eyes. "It's nice to meet you, and thanks for coming out. Consider supporting the Benson Galleries if you're in the market for art."

She walked away, the shadow of her bare ass under the sheer fabric of her dress swaying as she glided across the floor on wicked stilettos. The back slit of her dress opened almost to the crease of her curvy butt and I tightened my hand around the crystal stem of my champagne glass.

The food was delicious, yet it was ash in my mouth. What had I been thinking coming here? It was more than clear she didn't need me.

I could almost hear my friends jeering at me. *Are you a Dad Bod Dom or not? Pussy. Get your wife back. Be a goddamned dom.*

I ate a lobster pastry, grinning around the food as I stalked her with my eyes. *Booyah, motherfuckers.*

Natalie

Silently thanking Charles for his foresight, I drained the last of my club soda with lime. It looked enough like a cocktail no one said a word about me not drinking. Maybe I could indulge for my next show, but I promised myself I'd stay sober for this one.

The crowd was gone, along with the string quartet, leaving me with Charles and the cleaning crew. I couldn't believe the whole series had sold. Not only sold, but went to the same buyer who would display it as I intended. Maybe I ought to fly to DC to oversee the installation. I'd been invited, after all, and it was both poignant and satisfying to have my work hanging in a place that held such fond memories. Well, in the new club, anyway. It would have been great to have the paintings in Stronghold. I wondered if I should get in touch with Master Marshall from The Castle. I could create a Victorian series and…

I shook my head, knowing I was getting ahead of myself.

"Grab some food before they pack up the leftovers, sweetie," Charles urged, pushing me toward the buffet. "You haven't eaten a bite all night."

"Yes, Daddy. I'm going to change first before I spill anything on Eric's gorgeous dress."

Laughing, he shooed me into his office bathroom. I slipped the dress over my head and changed into the jeans and T-shirt I'd worn to my makeover. A good scrubbing took care of the carefully applied makeup.

Although I wanted color on my prematurely gray hair, my team of drag queen fairy godmothers refused, telling me silver was the new black. They weren't wrong. Instead of washing me out, the temporary streaks of purple and blue made me stylish and edgy, and I loved it. Hell, gray hair was trending on Instagram, and one of my photos had been hash-tagged *silverissexy* or some such nonsense.

The new La Perla thong over a fresh Brazilian wax made my girly bits very happy. I'd even dug into my jewelry box for the platinum ring that used to decorate my clit piercing, thanking my lucky stars the hole hadn't closed. Much, anyway. It still stung a bit. It wasn't like anyone was going to see it, but it made me feel beautiful and desirable again.

"Are you happy, Natalie?" Charles asked, handing me a plate when I rejoined him.

I took a bite of a crab-stuffed mushroom, my thoughts turning to the silver fox I'd met earlier. He looked so familiar, but I couldn't place where I'd seen him. Then again, with the black mask, he might have been Henry and I'd have never known it.

Of course, Henry wasn't nearly so impeccably groomed, and didn't wear suits.

"Yeah. Well, maybe I will be soon." I ate a toast point loaded with caviar, relishing the salty pop of fresh Beluga on my tongue. "Is it necessary that I be happy?"

"It's better than being medicated for depression," Charles replied, arching a groomed eyebrow. "Or lopping off an ear."

"True, that." I gave up on manners and picked up the bowl of caviar, along with the crackers and toast, then curled up in an overstuffed chair. "I guess I miss Henry, but I think I miss what used to be more than anything else."

He sat on the couch across from me with the tray of lobster pastries, transferring a few to my plate. "Understandable," he said gently. "Any hope of getting back to what used to be?"

I barked out a laugh and shook my head. "I doubt it. I'm honestly surprised he noticed I was gone."

"You were together for a long time. It must be hard to throw away almost twenty years of marriage."

"Maybe fifteen happy ones," I retorted, shoving my mouth full of caviar before I said anything else.

"That's more than a lot of people get."

"Fuck you, Charles." I ate the last pastry from the tray, then stood. "I'm out of here."

He laughed softly, taking no offense. "Okay. Call me in a few weeks to let me know how your new series is going."

"I already have the pieces outlined. I need to build the furniture, but they'll be done in a few months."

"That's wonderful, darling." Standing, he kissed my cheek. "Drive safe, and send me a text when you get home."

I rolled my eyes, secretly pleased that Charles seemed to care. "Yes, Daddy."

Walking outside, I stopped and inhaled the fresh evening air. A breeze blew off the river, bringing a chill with it. I shivered and strode down the alley to my car parked behind the gallery. Rummaging in my pocket for the fob, I clicked the button to unlock it, then fumbled the key ring, dropping it to the ground.

"Dammit." I bent down to grab my keys.

When I straightened, someone grabbed me from behind. Panicking, I tried to scream, but the sound was lost when my assailant slapped a piece of duct tape over my mouth and tugged a leather hood over my head.

Screaming behind the tape, I kicked out, but connected with nothing. Blinded, I couldn't defend myself and flailed my arms, desperately trying to escape.

I heard a curse, then my arms were wrenched behind my back and I heard the tearing sound of more tape as my attacker secured my wrists.

"Shhh, pretty doll," a digitized voice said as something metallic stroked my throat below the hood, icy against my skin. "If you're a good girl, you won't get hurt."

Whimpering behind the tape covering my mouth, I went limp, hoping he'd drop me so I could escape. My heart raced with terror when he picked me up. I couldn't breathe through the heavy mask and hot tears spilled from my eyes.

Stupid, stupid, stupid! Why hadn't I asked Charles to walk me out? What happened to my instincts? I knew better, and now I was going to die, the victim of some sick fuck who liked slicing up middle-aged women for shits and giggles.

My attacker popped the trunk on my car, then gently laid me inside, securing my ankles with more tape and a zip tie. The trunk closed, trapping me in darkness. I screamed again, the sound weak and thin through the tape. No one would hear me.

I wished I could go back a few days and tell Henry I loved him.

***

My face itched from drying tears and I was nauseous from the faint smell of exhaust in the close air of the trunk, but I almost didn't want the car to stop.

The first rule of personal safety was never let an attacker take you to a secondary location. I fucked that one up good, and had no idea where I was, much less what was going to happen when my assailant let me out. I didn't want to imagine it, worried it might make me panic again. Hysterics weren't my friend right now.

I tried to keep track of seconds at first, but lost focus, my brain conjuring all manner of crap I'd seen on true crime shows. Muscles cramping, I grimaced under the mask, unable to stretch in the tiny trunk. Cursing, I swore my next car would be a minivan or SUV with enough room to stretch out if I was ever kidnapped again.

The thought made me laugh hysterically behind the tape covering my mouth, but my breath caught when the car slowed and turned, bumping over gravel. A few moments later, the car stopped and I heard the sound of a garage door coming down before the engine shut off.

Stiffening when the car door slammed, I held my breath, but nothing happened. Another door opened and closed, sounding like one leading into a building or room. A few minutes later, I heard the door open and footsteps coming closer to the trunk.

The lid clicked then opened, sending a wash of cool air over my body. I had a few seconds to take a deep breath before my kidnapper lifted me from the trunk.

"Such a good girl," the digital voice crooned. "As long as you behave, I promise I won't hurt you."

CHAPTER THREE

Henry

Praying I hadn't been caught on video kidnapping my wife, I carried Natalie down the basement stairs, my back complaining with every step. She hadn't made it easy on me, and would have kicked my ass if I hadn't gotten that hood on her so quickly. There was definitely going to be some gym time in my future.

After activating the camera, I positioned her facing the St. Andrew's cross. Medical shears turned her T-shirt and jeans into ribbons, but I left the cute black thong in place. Natalie shivered, goosebumps forming on her pale skin when I traced the edges, dragging my fingers over the silk covering her mons.

It was funny how things came back, like muscle memory. It didn't matter how long it had been since I'd had Natalie at my mercy, my body remembered what to do. My cock thickened, straining against my zipper at the outward evidence of her fear.

"I'm going to cut the tape on your ankles now," I said softly, my distorted voice making her whimper behind the hood as I traced her car key down her spine to simulate the blade of a knife. "You're going to be a good girl for me, right?"

Without waiting for an answer, I sliced the tape, half expecting her to kick. To my satisfaction, she stayed perfectly still, her limbs stiff. Working quickly, I tightened the steel shackles around her ankles, then helped her catch her balance.

I watched her carefully, smirking when the muscles in her back clenched. "Such a pretty little doll," I murmured, dragging the key across the back of her neck. "Delicate and sweet with skin like silk, so easy to cut."

Muscles going lax, she held still while I cut the tape around her wrists, pulling it from her skin carefully so it didn't hurt her. Gently tugging her left arm up, I retrieved a cuff, relishing her whimper at the sound of metal closing around her wrist as I restrained her, then repeated the procedure for her free arm.

Watching her test her bonds, I turned the last item over in my hands. We hadn't used the steel training collar in years, a mistake I didn't intend to repeat. Ignoring her choked sob, I clasped it around her neck and secured it with a hex key, then laid a chain leash over her shoulder.

I collected her shredded clothes, scowling when her phone hit the floor. I swiped it awake and returned Charles's text, telling him Natalie had gotten home safely. That task completed, I turned it off and put it in my pocket, then filled a squeeze bottle with hot water from the sink in the bathroom. Hopefully, it would stay warm while we played.

Stripping off my jacket and tie, I adjusted myself in my tuxedo pants. Fuck, I didn't remember the last time I'd been so hard for my wife. She was so damned beautiful spread out on that cross, just waiting for me to feast. There was only one problem. I desperately wanted to see her face.

"Close your eyes, pretty doll. If you're a good girl and don't scream, I'll take the hood off."

Giving her a few seconds to follow my order, I grabbed a blindfold from our stash of toys, hoping it was clean. Taking a sniff, I decided it was good enough. I eased the hood away and tossed it to the floor, careful to stay behind her while I wrapped the blindfold around her eyes.

Her lips parting, Natalie inhaled, and I traced the key around her throat. "Ah ah," I murmured. "No screaming."

She pressed her lips together and nodded. Her hair tumbled free, making me itch to wrap it around my fist. Maybe tomorrow, I'd... No, I was getting ahead of myself. Lowering my head into her hair, I took a deep breath of her floral shampoo.

Looking at my beautiful wife and smelling her familiar perfume took me back in time, forcing me to remember what we'd shared. And what we'd lost. Aside from the possibility of parenthood, we'd lost each other.

Maybe kidnapping and terrorizing Natalie wasn't the best way to go about it. My friends would probably be horrified, but their wives were still where they belonged. As far as I was concerned, they didn't have any business judging me.

This wasn't a scene though. Natalie was terrified and I didn't like it. It went against everything I believed in to do this to her, but I had to show her what we once had. If this was the only way to get through to her, I'd accept the consequences.

"Do you know what safewords are, pretty doll?"

Her jaw tightening, she nodded.

"Use your words," I advised, letting the key move down her ribs to her thigh.

"Yes, asshole. I know what a fucking safe word is. Stupid son of a... Ouch! God damn it!"

I popped her ass harder than I probably should have, but I loved the pink handprint blossoming on the lower curve of her butt. "Such language," I murmured. "You may call me Master, and I want only a yes or no answer from you."

Giving her ass one last swat just to see her jump, I went to the wall rack holding my implements of pain and delight, choosing a suede flogger and a slim Delrin cane. It wasn't the harshest of my implements, but would still deliver enough sting to make Natalie mind her manners.

She'd call me Sir without batting an eye, but saying Master made her giggle and imitate Marty Feldman from *Young Frankenstein*. It used to irritate me, but she was so damned funny I'd eventually given up.

Wondering if she'd actually call me what I wanted, I tried again. "Do you know what a safeword is?"

"Yes…Master," she said, her teeth grinding together. "My safeword is red and I'm calling it, so let me go right now."

No, Natalie's safeword was *asparagus*. I almost reminded her, then remembered what I was supposed to be doing.

"Oh, pretty doll." I traced the key around her dusky peach nipple, delighted when it stiffened into a turgid bud. "You don't get a safeword tonight. You might get one after a few months, if you behave."

Natalie

The kidnapper stepped away and I let out a relieved breath. He hadn't hurt me, but I was terrified beyond reason. What had I been thinking to spout off like that? Granted, he hadn't done anything aside from a couple of slaps on my butt, but a smart kidnapping victim didn't call her assailant names, especially when he had a knife.

The thought of spending months like this... No. I refused to think about it. Someone would miss me. Eventually, maybe even Henry would wake up and wonder where I was.

"Master?" God, I hated that word. Henry and I used to laugh about it. He'd always wanted me to call him that when we played, but it made me giggle too much. I hitched in a sob, trying to keep the tears at bay.

Would it have killed me to give Henry another chance? I'd never have the opportunity now. Maybe I deserved what was happening to me. No, nobody deserved being assaulted and kidnapped, but it wouldn't have happened if I hadn't been stupid while leaving the gallery. If I'd taken a chance and told Henry about the show, he might have come with me. I could have tried, at least.

"What is it, pretty doll?" the man asked, his breath wafting across the back of my neck. He smelled like plain soap and starch, not unpleasant, but unfamiliar. It made me miss Henry's bay rum body wash with an ache that dug deep.

"What are you going to do to me?"

He went silent, the brush of the knife down my spine making me shudder.

"Master?"

"Good girl. I was waiting for you to address me properly." He dragged the blade across the underside of my breast, then up to my face, tracing my jaw with cold metal. "We're going to spend a few days together. Get to know each other. I want to learn what makes my pretty doll tick."

"What then, Master?" His digitized chuckle made me shiver and I bit back a whimper. "Please don't hurt me," I whispered, terror bringing tears to my eyes.

"We'll see." He petted my belly with a warm palm, caressing and gentle, then pushed his fingers into my panties.

I stiffened and let out a soft cry, tears dampening the blindfold when his searching fingers found the ring piercing the hood of my clit.

"Such a naughty little doll," the mechanical voice crooned. "Only bad girls put rings in their pussies."

Oh God, what was he going to do? My stomach heaved at the thought of the horrifying punishments he might come up with. "No, please, Master! I don't—"

"Naughty little dolls with clit piercings always need a good spanking, but I think you might need something extra to remind you of the lesson."

He removed his hand, and I heard the soft step of his shoe, then a refrigerator opening and closing before he returned to me. He twitched my thong aside and something cold touched my asshole.

"Relax, pretty doll. I'm not going to hurt you… yet."

This wasn't my first rodeo with anal. It used to be one of Henry's favorite games. I exhaled, forcing myself to let the object in. Whatever he was pushing into my ass would hurt less if I could convince my body to accept it. The object was small, maybe the width of a couple of fingers, certainly nothing I needed to fuss over, but my core spasmed, clenching around the intrusion.

"There we go," he said, removing his hand. "Let's get you warmed up."

I shuddered and more tears soaked the blindfold. Henry used to say that right before our play sessions.

There was a whoosh of air a second before leather tails struck my shoulders. Although it didn't hurt, the pop of sound made me flinch.

Obviously skilled, he worked the flogger in a figure eight, carefully avoiding the vulnerable area over my kidneys. My flesh warmed and despite my fear, I relaxed into the familiar sensation of a gentle flogging. I couldn't remember the last time I'd been under the care of a talented whip thrower. Henry had been so good at it. I bit back a sob just thinking of him.

Yet the burning in my ass grew stronger, worsening when I clenched around it. I bit my lip to hold in a cry of discomfort, determined not to give my kidnapper the satisfaction. Even worse, I was actually beginning to enjoy the heat.

"Please, Master…" I choked back a cry as I clenched around the searing object in my ass. "Let me go. My husband—"

He stopped and I heard the sound of something hitting the floor a second before the blade of his knife traced spirals over my ribs. "I don't see a wedding ring, pretty doll. Do you know what happens to naughty girls who lie to their Masters?"

"Please, I'm not lying!"

He tsked and traced my jaw with the blade, making me shudder. "We'll just have to fix it so you can't do it again, won't we?" The knife disappeared and he pressed something cold and metal against my lips. "Open that pretty, lying mouth, sweetheart."

I turned my face away, closing my mouth. A whistle sounded an instant before a line of fire lit up the center of my ass, and I screamed at the combination of the cane stroke and the burn inside me. Grabbing my hair, he pushed a ring gag into my mouth, spreading my lips obscenely wide as he buckled it behind my head.

"Naughty little dolls get caned," the digitized voice hissed. "They get caned thoroughly while their bottoms are full of ginger, then they get skull-fucked so they remember not to tell lies."

Shudders wracked my body, and I let out an animalistic cry around the gag as I yanked on the metal cuffs holding my wrists. The thought of someone forcing me... No, this wasn't going to happen. The cuffs didn't give, and I screamed again, desperate to get away.

"Are you crying, pretty doll?" he asked, tracing a finger down my cheek. "I like it when you cry. Your tears make my cock hard, so I'm going to reward you for it."

Even if I dared ask, the ring gag prevented speech. I didn't want to know what he considered a reward and it wasn't as if anything I said would stop him. He tugged my thong aside, exposing my pussy, then pushed something against my clit before replacing the silk over my mound. The object buzzed, making me jerk and cry out.

My clit was so damned sensitive, and I cursed myself for replacing my piercing. I didn't want to come for him. Not like this, and not for someone who wasn't Henry. Unfortunately, I didn't think I could stop it. Despite my terror, sensation was already rising in my belly, the vibrations against my clit ring making moisture trickle down my thigh.

Laughing softly, he turned up the vibration. "Oh, very nice. Let's try an experiment, shall we? I want to see how long I can cane you before you come."

The first stripe lit up the upper curve of my bottom, making me flinch and inadvertently tighten around the ginger in my ass. God, that fucking burned. Henry had always teased me with figging, but we'd never tried it. I whimpered softly and let my head fall. He'd have loved it, the sadist.

Again, and again, the cane delivered stinging pain as my kidnapper worked it methodically down the fleshy mounds of my backside, never striking twice in the same place. The toy buzzed madly against my clit and I bucked my hips, tightening on the ginger once more.

The burn changed into throbbing heat, pulsing in counterpoint to the toy as he delivered a stroke to the sensitive crease where my ass met my thighs.

God, if the man wielding the cane had been my husband, I'd already be begging for more. Everything he was doing seemed specifically designed to tap into my darkest desires Henry used to feed with such devastating skill. My belly clenched against the orgasm barreling down on me. It was going to happen whether I wanted it or not.

When the cane bit into my upper thighs, I screamed and let go, sobbing out my pain and fear as my core spasmed, rocking me to my soul.

CHAPTER FOUR

Henry

I hooked the strap of the cane around my belt, letting it dangle from my hip. God, Natalie was gorgeous when she came.

She collapsed, sagging in her bonds. I freed the cuffs from the cross, leaving them on her wrists and ankles. My cock throbbed against her cute ass, making me clench my teeth. It wasn't time for me to make love to her like I wanted. We weren't ready.

I wasn't done, not by a long shot. I let her fall to her knees, then crouched to secure her wrists behind her back. Unzipping my pants, I freed my cock and quickly removed my piercing before grabbing her blue and purple streaked silver hair. That metal ring would tell her louder than words who I was, and I wasn't ready.

A ribbon of drool trickled down her chin from the ring gag, making my balls ache with need. Tugging gently, I pulled her up, tightening my fist in her hair.

"Do you remember what I told you, pretty doll?" I asked, brushing her lips with the tip of my hard shaft.

Natalie grunted around the gag and made a halfhearted attempt to escape, then nodded.

"Good girl." I eased my cock into her warm mouth, sinking both hands into her hair to hold her still while I fucked her face with long, leisurely strokes, too afraid of nutting to fuck her like I wanted.

I wasn't seventeen anymore, and my recovery time wasn't what it used to be.

She gasped and choked, viscous spit streaming down her chest. I thrust into her throat, holding her nose closed with one hand.

"How long can you go without air, pretty doll?" I asked, my dick filling her throat. My eyes rolled back and I gritted my teeth at the vibrations from her breathless whines.

The only thing that would make this scene perfect would have been the sight of her wide, terrified eyes, but that would come soon. I wasn't ready to reveal myself yet.

Letting out a groan of pleasure, I allowed the edges of Natalie's teeth to scrape against my cock, knowing she couldn't bite down. Ring gags, for the win. I'd always loved having Natalie at my mercy. Bound and helpless to my whims. Why had I let us grow so far apart? Never again. I jerked away, stroking my throbbing cock until I spilled cum to the floor in front of her.

Natalie coughed, choking for air as spit spilled down her chin. She'd never looked so beautiful. I unfastened the buckle holding the gag in place and tossed it to the side. Fisting her hair, I pushed her face to the floor, hardening myself against her whimpers. "Clean up the mess, pretty doll," I ordered, holding her down with a leather dress shoe in the middle of her shoulders while I zipped my pants. Thankfully, the voice distortion device hid the roughness of my words.

She hesitated, stiffening against my hold, then her tongue touched the floor, lapping at my cum. Her pretty silver hair flowed over her shoulders, held back by the blindfold, and her ass blossomed with bruising red stripes from the cane. She didn't get it all, but I wasn't willing to remove the blindfold so she could see the last few drops.

Fuck, she was so damned hot, but there was one thing I forgot.

"Stay," I barked, leaving her hunched on the concrete floor while I retrieved the squeeze bottle. Thankfully, it was still warm enough for my purposes. My lips curled into an evil grin and I strode back to her.

Watersports had always been one of Natalie's few hard limits. She'd eventually figure out it was just water, but I could hardly wait to see her reaction. I unzipped my trousers again, smirking at her flinch. To my shock, my cock was already hardening again.

I rested my foot on her leash to keep her still, then upended the bottle and squeezed, sending a stream of warm water over her back.

Screaming hoarsely, she jerked, pulling a few inches of chain out from under my shoe. I settled my weight firmly and finished emptying the bottle before zipping my pants.

Natalie curled into a ball, and I hardened myself against her crying. Tonight was for teaching her a lesson. Tomorrow, her training would begin in earnest. She would be furious when I finally revealed myself to her, but it was worth it.

I reached down and unfastened the chain from her wrist cuffs, then picked up her leash. "Come on, filthy doll. It's time for me to put my toy away for the evening," I said, giving the leash a gentle tug. "We have a busy day tomorrow."

Still crying softly, she wrapped her arms around her knees and didn't move.

I pulled the cane free and let it fly, careful to

place the blow in a narrow bit of unmarked flesh on her ass.

Letting out a little screech of pain, she tried to scramble away, her teeth bared between swollen lips. "Fuck you!"

"I meant now, sweetheart. Get on your knees and crawl next to my leg like a good girl. I'd hate to have to punish you again, especially since you're already going to get a caning tomorrow for your language."

Her mouth twisted into a snarl. "Fine," she spat. "If I'm going to take the punishment anyway, you're a sick, sad little fuckwit who can't get a woman without kidnapping her. You're a foul, disgusting piece of—"

"I think I might have a penis gag in my bag of tricks," I murmured, cutting her off. "Care to rephrase that?"

Natalie straightened on her knees, her back rigid. "How careless of me. You're a foul, disgusting piece of shit, Master."

I bit back a laugh and tugged on the leash, bringing her to my side. There was my Natalie. I'd give her this small triumph. "Come along, pet. It's time for bed."

Keeping my pace slow in deference to her knees on the concrete, I took her to the bathroom. "You have two minutes to wash and take care of business."

Feeling around, her hand brushed against the toilet and she stood. "Can you at least turn around?"

"Nope. Pee now, or you'll have to hold it all night."

"Asshole," she muttered under her breath.

Smirking, I watched her attend to her needs and wash her hands. "There's a toothbrush and toothpaste to your right," I advised. "You'll drink a bottle of water when you finish."

"May I have a shower, Master?"

Giving her butt a fond squeeze, I said, "Good girl, but no. Maybe tomorrow. You should hurry if you want to brush your teeth."

The thought of being covered in piss must be driving her nuts. Although I was surprised she hadn't figured out I'd used water, I wasn't about to tell her.

When she finished and drank her water, I pushed her to her knees once more and led her to the cage under the bondage bed, wondering if she remembered it. She'd loved it if I didn't leave her in there too long. The reinforcement of my dominance used to settle her when nothing else would, but it had been years since she'd been in it.

I opened the door, watching with satisfaction when she flinched at the sound of metal clanking. "Face on the floor and hold your ass cheeks apart for me," I ordered.

She chewed on the idea for a few seconds, then gritted her teeth and obeyed, revealing the ginger still plugging her ass. Reaching down, I pulled it out, then slapped her backside.

"Get in, then turn around and put your hands through the bars."

"Why?"

I didn't answer, waiting for her to come up with the appropriate address. Instead of asking properly, she grunted and crawled carefully into the cage, her hands and knees sinking into the soft mattress. When her ankles cleared the door, I shut it behind her, grinning at her flinch of surprise.

"Hands, now," I barked.

She jumped and turned in the cage, bumping her head on the top. Cursing softly, she pushed her wrists through the bars. Thankfully, they were just wide enough apart to permit the passage of her cuffs. I hadn't thought to check. Crouching, I secured them with a short piece of chain, snapping a padlock through the connection so she couldn't free herself or remove her blindfold.

"Sleep well, pretty doll. You have a big day tomorrow."

After checking to make sure the camera was still recording, I walked up the stairs, locking the door behind me. She was secure enough, and wasn't bound to the point she'd need to be supervised, but I'd keep an eye on her from my computer just in case.

I couldn't wait for morning. Tomorrow was going to b glorious.

Natalie

My butt ached and I itched. I couldn't believe that asshole had peed on me. That so wasn't my kink. I let Henry do it once, but only in the shower, and only after he promised to let me bathe right after. Thankfully, he hadn't enjoyed it enough to do it again.

The thought of having to spend the night with someone's urine on my body made my belly churn, but I pushed the nausea down. There wasn't much I could do about it except pray he let me wash tomorrow. At least it didn't stink yet, but the strong odor of bleach-based cleaner suffusing the room might be covering it.

Tears pricked in my eyes and were absorbed by the blindfold. Already clammy and damp, it stuck to my face, making me wish I could take it off. Unfortunately, with my hands chained outside the bars, I couldn't even scratch my fucking nose.

At least I could lie down, and the padded mattress wasn't too uncomfortable. I tried to rest, my mind whirling at my circumstances.

Had this been a crime of opportunity, or had I been targeted? What did he hope to gain? I couldn't make sense of anything. None of what he did had been consensual. Even my orgasm had been dragged kicking and screaming from my body and I hated myself for it. Yet he hadn't truly harmed me.

It would have been so easy for him to hurt me. One slip of that knife blade or a few harder blows with that damned cane might have scarred me. Or worse. Yet he hadn't. Hell, Henry and I had done more intense scenes back in the day. Everything was too confusing and I couldn't think. I rested my head on outstretched arms and tried to get comfortable. If I had any hope of getting free, I needed to sleep.

God, I missed Henry so badly it was a physical ache deeper than the cane marks on my bottom. If I managed to get out of this, I would go back to him and try to fix what was broken between us. Maybe he wouldn't listen or care, but I owed it to us both to try. The thought gave me a little comfort and I drifted into an uneasy doze.

The sound of a door slamming jerked me from sleep. Still muzzy and confused, it took me a moment to figure out where I was. Heavy footsteps pounded down wood stairs and I stilled.

"Good morning, pet," he called cheerfully in that creepy digitized voice. "If you behave, I'll have your breakfast ready in a few minutes."

There were several beeps, then I heard the low hum of a microwave before his footsteps came closer.

"You're supposed to thank your Master," he murmured, still in that awful voice.

The threat was clear. If I didn't, I might not get a chance to eat. My stomach tumbled at the smell of bacon wafting through the room. "Thank you, Master."

My voice broke on the last word, but he didn't appear to notice as he freed my hands and unlocked the cage door. Picking up my leash, he tugged on it. I didn't bother to try standing and crawled next to him, the concrete icy under my knees. When my hands brushed against something soft, I stopped.

"Just a little further," he encouraged. "You've been a good girl, so I have a cushion for you to kneel on while you eat."

"Thank you, Master." I said the words mechanically, but they came out. He rewarded me with a soft pat on the head, making me bite my tongue against another curse. Moving forward, I held back a sigh of relief at the soft pillow under me. At my age, crawling on concrete wasn't the most pleasant thing to do.

Metal clanked when he dropped my chain, then I heard something being set on the floor. "Your food is in front of you. I hope you enjoy it."

Of course, he'd make me eat off the floor. What the hell else had I expected? I felt around for a napkin and flatware, but came up empty. "May I have a fork, Master?"

"Maybe someday," he murmured. "After you're trained properly."

I found the bowl with my hands and lowered my face to it, swearing to all the gods in the universe that someday I'd wrap a chain around my captor's neck and squeeze until his head popped off.

The scrambled eggs, laden with cheese and crumbled bacon, were surprisingly good and I was starving. Within minutes the bowl was empty, but my face was covered with scraps of food. Laughing softly, he cleaned me up and allowed me a few sips of coffee with light cream and no sugar, just how I liked it.

How had he known that? Had he been stalking me? The thought sent a chill down my spine and I wondered if he'd hurt Henry. I considered asking, but was too afraid of mentioning it. He didn't believe I was married anyway, and it was probably safer not to say a word.

Without waiting for him to prompt me, I said, "Thank you for breakfast, Master."

"Such a good girl," he crooned, the electronically altered voice buzzing. "It's time to get you clean and ready for the day."

He picked up the leash and I followed him on my hands and knees, too excited at the prospect of a shower to ask questions. I smelled the scent of plain soap as he helped me stand. "Bend over and spread your cheeks, pretty doll."

Ugh. Not again. What the hell was he going to shove up my butt this time? Cool, slippery lube trickled over my asshole, making me shiver, then he eased something hard into me and I heard a clatter of metal on metal. Whatever he'd used was small. I hadn't even had to relax much, and couldn't imagine what he'd…

Flinching, I cried out when warm liquid filled my bowels. He was giving me a fucking enema? Granted, it wasn't my first one. I used to do it all the time when I played with Henry, but the thought of sharing that intimacy with a kidnapper sickened me to my core.

I considered trying to escape, but he still had a

firm grip on the leash and it wasn't likely he'd left the door at the top of the stairs unlocked. Besides, my gut was already aching from the pressure. He must have used one of the old-fashioned bags instead of the disposable ones from the drugstore.

He laid a hand on my hip. "We'll leave this in for a few minutes to make sure you're all sparkly clean inside. You can have a shower later."

Fuck you. "Yes, master."

I bit back a hysterical giggle. Hearing that always made me think of my favorite movie, *Young Frankenstein.*

It's Frahnkensteen!

I didn't think I'd find that movie funny ever again.

"I'm going to pull it out now," he said, his voice filled with warning. "I recommend you don't make a mess."

Biting back a whimper, I clenched, desperate to keep the liquid inside until I could get to the toilet. Once the nozzle was free, I sat quickly and sighed in relief. I hated him watching me do something so private, but was too desperate to protest–not that he'd have listened. When I finished, I cleaned myself up, then washed my hands.

Before I could beg for a shower, he said, "Good girl. Bend over again for me. I have a present for you."

Thankfully, the blindfold hid my rolling eyes. I obeyed, spreading my cheeks wide for whatever horror he had planned. More lube trickled down my crack, cold and slippery. With Henry, anal play had been fun and sexy. With the creepy fuckwit, it was twisted and made me sick to my stomach.

The plug was large, and I wasn't used to

something so big anymore. It had been a long time for me, but I held in a whine of discomfort and tried to relax.

"How does that feel?" he asked, stroking my backside once the plug was fully seated.

"It's fine, Master." As if I'd tell him otherwise. Something dragged across my inner thigh, making me wonder if the plug had a tail attached.

"Good." He tugged the leash down, making me drop to my knees. "Come along. I have a surprise for you."

He led me from the bathroom, then helped me into a wooden chair. Although my weight pressed the plug deeper into my ass, maybe things were looking up if he was allowing me to sit somewhere other than the floor.

"Hands behind you, pretty doll."

Or maybe not. Grimacing, I let him chain my wrists together behind the back of the chair. My ankles got the same treatment, forcing me to spread my legs so my hips didn't lock up.

He stroked my hair, then fumbled with the knot on the blindfold before pulling it away. Bright lights blinded me and I blinked tears away until my vision cleared. Air stalled in my throat and I couldn't drag it into my lungs at the sight of a painfully familiar basement. *My* basement. *Oh, God. Henry!*

CHAPTER FIVE

Henry

The expression on Natalie's face was a priceless mix of horror and shock. I'd been waiting all night to see her reaction and she didn't disappoint.

"You fucking bastard," she hissed, trying to turn to see me. "What did you do to my husband? I swear to God, if you hurt him…"

That was her first thought? She worried about me instead of herself? Fuck. What was I supposed to do? All my carefully laid plans seemed cruel and unnecessary now. I was leaning toward ending the whole charade, but didn't think it would gain us a damned thing. After almost twenty years together, I knew my wife, and she was going to be spitting mad. Yet warmth blossomed in my chest at the proof she still cared.

Screaming in fury, she struggled, nearly overturning the chair. "I'm going to fucking kill you!"

No, I had to stay the course. It was the only way to regain her submission and restore our marriage. Pulling off the voice synthesizer, I moved around the chair and crouched in front of her. "Natalie, calm down."

"God damn you! I…" She blinked and looked up. "Henry? What happened to your hair?"

"Haircut. Are you done yelling?"

Her eyes narrowed, a frown wrinkling the skin

between her eyes. "Oh, my God. That *was* you in the gallery! What the hell is going on? Get these cuffs off me right now."

"No."

"What the fuck do you mean, no? Let me go."

"Not until you listen."

"Did you do this? Are you the asshole who locked me in my own damned trunk and kidnapped me?" Her face reddened as her voice rose to a shout. Thankfully, we didn't have any neighbors close by. Mrs. Jacobsen's place was almost two hundred yards away and across the road. Aside from that, she was deaf as a post.

"Yes. You're safe, but—"

"Henry," she said, her voice going dangerously soft. "Let me go. Now."

I pulled out the remote for the e-stim plug in her ass and thumbed the button to activate it. Jerking, she shrieked and arched her back. Easing the power down, I said, "You're going to sit still and listen to me."

"Or what?" Challenge flared in her eyes.

My dick pulsed and I had to focus to control my reaction. One of the things I'd always loved best about Natalie was her willingness to stand up to me. She didn't back down. Well, not usually. She'd given up on our marriage quickly enough.

"You're going to listen, or you're going to ride that electric butt plug until you pass out," I replied, keeping my voice smooth and calm. "But first, you're going to watch something."

She pressed her lips together, then gave me an abrupt nod. "Will you let me go after that?"

"No."

"Henry, I—"

I touched the controller for the butt plug, making her hiss out a breath and squirm in her chair. "Be a good girl and watch."

Grabbing the remote for the television, I turned it on and played back the captured video from the night before, watching her instead of the screen.

Her eyes widened and she paled. "My own damned car key. You made me think it was a knife. You fucking—"

I tapped the controller again. She squeaked, but went silent. "Yes. And watch your language. We're getting to the best part."

On the screen, Natalie went to her knees, hands bound behind her to accept my cock in her mouth. "You look so beautiful," I murmured, stroking her hair. "So perfectly submissive."

She watched silently, her face unreadable, then closed her eyes when I spilled my cum to the floor.

"Ah ah," I said, zapping her again. "Open those beautiful eyes and watch."

"Asshole," she whispered, her eyes fixed on the screen once more as the scene played out. "Water... That wasn't piss. You tricked me into—"

"I know your hard limits, sweetheart." I paused the video and set the remote aside.

"Great. That's just fucking awesome," she snapped. "I found a new hard limit, thanks to you. I'm calling red on being kidnapped by the husband I am definitely divorcing."

I pressed the controller again, giving her a somewhat stronger jolt. "Don't you remember, pretty doll? You don't get a safeword. Besides, your safeword isn't red."

Twitching, she glared at the device in my hand. "Don't call me that."

"Here's what's going to happen," I replied, speaking over her. "You're going to get exactly what you wanted. We're going to talk. I am going to touch you, and we are definitely going to make love."

"Yeah, in your dreams," she muttered.

Judging by the fury and hurt on her face, I needed to bend for her. Well, for this one thing anyway. She wasn't going to come to heel for anything but an abject apology, and she deserved an explanation. Crouching, I dropped to my knees at her feet.

"I'm sorry. Everything you said in your letter was right. I let us drift apart. As much as I want to blame my job, I can't. It was me, because I didn't know what to say."

The faint lines around her mouth tightened. "*Hello, how was your day* would have been a start."

"I tried. I made that spare room into a game room, hoping to entice you into playing with me again." I stroked her knee, relishing the smooth skin under my palm. "Do you remember how you used to whip my butt in Mario Kart?"

She looked away, but a reluctant smile blossomed on her lips. "Yeah, then you would whip *my* butt for beating you." Her smile fading, she added, "That room was supposed to have been a nursery, Henry. You didn't even ask me before remodeling. I thought… Never mind."

"What did you think?"

"I thought it was your way of distancing yourself from me. You hid up there, and I…I didn't feel welcome."

"I wanted you to come in, but you never did. Why?"

"You never asked, dumbass." She bit her lip, obviously expecting another jolt. In a softer tone, she added, "Every time I looked in that room, it reminded me of what I couldn't have."

"I'm sorry. I should have talked to you first."

Natalie nodded, then met my eyes. "So, what do we do now? You can't keep me down here forever."

"Wanna bet?"

Letting out a dry laugh, she shook her head. "You'll have to go back to work eventually."

"I took the twenty and out retirement after my boss gave my project to a twenty-five-year-old kid, then expected me to train her to take over. You were right about that too." I stood and tipped up her chin to make her look at me. "We're going to stay down here until we get back to where we were."

"And where's that?" she snapped. "Are you talking about the part where we were roommates who happen to have joint bank accounts and a marriage certificate? Have to say, I'm not interested."

I traced a thumb over the controller, trying to resist the urge to give her another jolt of electricity. My kidnapping plan wasn't working the way I'd hoped. Hell, I wasn't sure what I expected, but Natalie's animosity wasn't really surprising. I'd just have to work with what we had and hope for the best.

"No. We're going to start over, beginning with your training."

"What on earth are you talking about?"

"I'm going to teach you how to be submissive again. You're going to relearn what you've forgotten."

"I haven't forgotten shit, Henry! If you—"

Grimly, I thumbed the controller to its highest setting, watching impassively while she writhed, screeching in pain. After counting to five, I turned it down. "Natalie, this is going to happen. You might not remember how to be a slave, but I know how to be a Master."

I pinched her nipple until tears popped in her eyes. "And this time, you *will* call me Master."glorious.

Natalie

"Fuck you, Henry," I spat. "If you want to talk, then talk. I'm not playing with you."

Although he was still wearing the ragged concert T-shirt and boxers he usually wore to bed, his new haircut and beard trim made him look amazing. Between the tuxedo and the fashionable hair, it was no wonder I hadn't recognized him at the gallery.

He fingered the controller and an evil smile lit up his handsome face. That smile reminded me of the man he used to be. The sadist he used to be. And maybe the woman I once was too.

"I said nothing about playing. This isn't a game, pretty doll."

He stepped behind me and the plug in my ass warmed, the itchy burn of an electrical charge growing inside me. Pressing my lips together, I refused to answer. To my surprise, he didn't zap me again. At low power, the plug made my core twitch with want and my pussy dampened. Now that the abject terror was gone, I could relax. Well, maybe. Henry still hadn't let me go. Was he serious about keeping me down here until I agreed to his terms? I twitched with a mixture of arousal and trepidation.

We'd played kidnapping games a time or six back in the day. Wooded and private, our property was perfect for outdoor entertainments. I loved the chase back then, and especially liked it when he caught me.

I'd loved him so hard. A big part of me still did and always would. Yet I didn't know if I could trust him to stay. I might have been the one to physically leave, but he'd checked out emotionally long ago and I didn't think I could take it a second time.

All the promises I made to myself when I thought I was in the hands of a madman ran through my head, but this wasn't at all what I expected.

Be careful what you wish for.

As if to reward me, Henry stroked my hair. "Good girl," he murmured.

"Please, let me go. I'll take a shower and we'll go upstairs and talk about this. We also need to delete that video."

He kept petting me, his hand moving across the back of my neck to my shoulder. "Do you remember my favorite game?"

"The original Call of Duty."

"I'm crushed," he replied, his fingers moving down my arm to brush against the side of my breast. "You don't remember orgasm poker?"

Oh. Fuck. I shifted, trying to hide an involuntary shudder. "I never liked that game," I replied, keeping my face set in what I hoped was an expressionless mask.

Tugging on my hair, he pulled my head back, then leaned close. His warm breath brushing my ear made goosebumps dance across my flesh. "Are you sure about that? I used to think you'd lose on purpose just so I'd edge you."

There was no way I was going to tell Henry he was right. "No, I just suck at poker. You didn't answer my question."

He chuckled softly and stroked a lazy hand down my breastbone. "You didn't ask one."

"I told you to—"

"Ah ah," he said, pinching my nipple hard enough to make me suck in a harsh breath. "You told. You didn't ask. You also forgot to call me Master."

Biting back a whimper, I wrenched my body to the side in an attempt to make him let go. "Henry, please."

"That's better, but I think you need a reminder of who you are." Thankfully, he released my tender breast.

My nipple throbbing, I bit back a snarky comment. "Who do you think I am?"

"You're my wife." He wrapped the blindfold around my head. "And I love you very much."

Tears welled in my eyes behind the thick cloth. Dammit. Henry didn't play fair at all. Without the benefit of sight, I couldn't help but remember how things used to be. No matter what happened at work, the weekends were ours. We used to connect with each other in the most intimate ways possible. Fifteen glorious years of devotion, gone.

He stroked my cheek, a single glancing touch almost too gentle to be felt. The sound of his footsteps echoed across the concrete floor and I heard him open our toy cupboard.

"Henry?"

Instead of answering, he continued rummaging through our toys. Gritting my teeth, I tried again. "Master?"

He moved closer and brushed his hand across my shoulders. "Good girl. What's your question?"

Asshole. "Why now?"

"You'll have to be more specific, pet."

"Why did you kidnap me? Why have you all of a sudden decided you want to be a Master again when we haven't had a relevant conversation in years?"

"I—"

"Are you jealous that someone else might have

been playing with your toys while you ignored them?" I spilled everything I hadn't wanted to say, the words flowing like poison from an infection. "Will you go back to pretending I don't exist if I give in? Are you—"

He pinched my nose, forcing me to open my mouth. I gagged and swallowed as the thick silicone of a penis gag pressed on my tongue. In a flash, Henry had it buckled at the back of my head, preventing me from spitting it out.

Stroking tangled hair off my face, he said, "Yes, I am jealous. I'm jealous you made such a success at something you've always dreamed of doing. I'm also incredibly proud of you for taking the chance on yourself, and I wish I'd been by your side to celebrate with you. I'm jealous of every man who saw you in that black lace dress, but you've never looked more beautiful."

He cupped my jaw and kissed my forehead. "I'm not going to let you go without a fight, Natalie. We're going to stay in this basement until our relationship is back where it would have been if I hadn't been an idiot."

His hand left my face and stroked my breastbone, moving down my belly to the piercing. "I thought I'd never see this again. I'm glad you put it back where it belongs."

Giving it a gentle tap, he asked, "Do you remember when you got it? I got my Prince Albert at the same time and we helped each other take care of them until they healed."

I choked back a sob and nodded. I couldn't believe he remembered that. A second later, I heard the low hum of our vibrating wand and stiffened as the toy touched me. The plug in my ass warmed, sending shards of tingling sensation deep into my core.

Damn him. Henry knew just where to touch me with the wand. He hadn't forgotten a single one of my hot buttons or my hard and soft limits. Aside from the pretend urine, he hadn't done a single thing I would have safeworded over. If I'd realized my car key was held by someone I trusted, it would have been a deliciously erotic experience.

Something touched my nipple and I choked around the penis gag as he pinched it between the jaws of a clamp. Another surge of electricity coursed into my body through the tender bud. Whimpering, I tried to jerk away, but couldn't avoid the bite of the second clamp or the matching jolt of current waxing and waning in tandem with the plug in my ass.

Henry was an expert at walking the thin line between pleasure and pain. He must be delighted with these new instruments of hedonistic torture.

Please don't let him edge me.

Slick arousal cooled on my pussy and I arched for more contact with the maddening toy brushing my clit, but he pulled it away.

I bit back a low whine, knowing what was coming. My heart thundered in my chest, partly in fear, but mostly with anticipation.

Stroking my hair, he bent to nip the delicate skin under my ear. "Why didn't you remind me? We can't have a proper session without music."

He settled headphones over my ears and the thumping notes of his favorite *play* list stole the last of my senses.

Oh, God.

CHAPTER SIX

Henry

Natalie's skin glistened with sweat. Mute, deafened aside from the music, and blind, she looked like my next greatest meal, and I couldn't wait to feast. First, I had to remind her how good it could be. I was more than aware I'd lost Natalie's trust, but I was determined to get it back. All I had to do was prove I was still the man she loved.

As much as I wanted to save the video for posterity, I turned the camera off. She'd never learn to trust me again if she thought there was a video of our scene.

Failure was untenable and I refused to believe she didn't love me. She might be furious, but she'd tried to defend me when she thought I'd been harmed. The memory sent a warm thrill through my chest.

The last thing I wanted to do was cause her pain. Sensual agony was another story, and I was more than ready to make her come until she screamed for mercy. I had to watch her carefully though. She was helpless and without a way to communicate a safeword. Although I told her she wouldn't get one, I wasn't about to push her further than she could go. My inner sadist was content with letting her think it.

Increasing the power to the clamps on her nipples, I touched the vibrating wand to her clit. Nearly dislodging the headphones, she tossed her head back and cried out around the penis gag. Her chest flushed pink, the gorgeous blush traveling up her neck as she strained toward her climax.

I pulled the toy away and traced circles around her navel, easing her down for a few seconds before moving it back to her clit. Grinning savagely, I thumbed the control to the butt plug, bumping the e-stim higher.

Screeching around the gag, she thrashed in her bonds, her hips bucking lewdly. Tendons strained in her neck and her face turned bright red.

"I can't decide if I like the electric toys or the ginger better," I said, knowing Natalie couldn't hear me. "Maybe one of these days, I'll use them at the same time."

Unfortunately, her rasping breaths combined with the red flush on her face and chest meant she was nearing the edge of her endurance. I lowered the power on the electric toys, then ground the vibrating wand against her clit, circling the tender, swollen flesh until she cried out and her body spasmed. She jerked hard, making the chair creak under her as she sobbed her pleasure.

Still panting, she collapsed, her body quivering. I wiped a trickle of drool from her chin, then eased the first clamp away from her nipple, rubbing the abused nub firmly to ease the sting. By the time I had the rest of the toys removed and put in a plastic tub for cleaning, my balls ached with need.

I wanted nothing more than to take Natalie to bed and fuck her to another screaming orgasm. Snorting out a laugh, I pulled the gag from her swollen mouth and wiped her face with a handkerchief. At my age, I'd need some of those little blue pills if I intended to do it without mechanical help. These days, my speed was more gentle lovemaking and a good night's sleep than the all-day scenes we'd once shared.

That didn't make it bad, just different. It was something we were going to have to get used to. Of course, Mother Nature, in her infinitely bitchy sense of humor, had women reaching their sexual peak about the same time men were finding their favorite recliners.

I pulled the headphones free of her tangled hair. The blue and purple streaks suited her. It was a pity they'd likely wash out.

She blinked at me, her eyes glazed. "I thought you were going to edge me," she croaked.

"No, not today, pet." I unbuckled the restraints, then walked her into the bathroom. I started the shower, helping her into the fiberglass enclosure after I tested the water temperature. Dropping my T-shirt and boxers in a heap on the floor, I joined her.

Although her shoulders stiffened, she didn't protest and allowed me to wash her from head to toe, easing her tense muscles with a gentle massage. Her knees were reddened from crawling across the concrete, making me wish I'd thought to lay down a rug or something.

Should I get started with her training, or let her rest for the remainder of the day? It was barely noon, but I didn't want to give Natalie too much time to think up more arguments. More than anything, she needed to remember how it had been between us.

After rinsing the last of the soap from her hair, I turned off the taps, then grabbed a thick towel from the stack on a shelf above the toilet and dried her carefully.

Her eyes drifted closed and she leaned against me. I resisted the urge to dance a jig. If she felt comfortable enough to let me support her, maybe things were looking up. "It's time for a short nap," I murmured. "You can sleep in bed with me, or in your cage."

Natalie looked up and met my eyes, but didn't answer for several seconds. She pulled away, taking a few steps back. "I'll take the cage."

"Fair enough," I replied, keeping my voice calm. I wasn't about to let her see my disappointment. Maybe I'd asked too much, too quickly. I should have cuffed her to the wrought iron bed frame and forced the issue, but I'd already offered her the choice.

Then again, giving her a little space might work in my favor. I had to show her I cared about her feelings and would let her come to me in her own time.

Natalie wasn't the only one who needed a D/s refresher course. I'd completely forgotten how to be a dom. The only difference between me and my wife was determination to see this through. It was almost like starting over with a brand new submissive. What other dom got a chance to have a fresh start with the love of his life? Well, aside from Ray, Faris, and Logan anyway.

Maybe she just needed a little motivation. My lips twitching into a feral smile, I put a hand on her shoulder, meaning to push her to her knees. "In that case, you're going to crawl."

Natalie

"I need a moment, please."

Henry left the bathroom without comment, and even allowed me to close the door. Resting my hands on the sink, I stared at myself in the mirror. God, I looked like shit. I had sex hair and my lips were swollen from that damned penis gag. My face was blotchy and the bags under my eyes looked like full-sized steamer trunks.

Turning away, I propped a foot on the toilet lid and removed the butt plug, scowling at the evil thing. Then again, at low power, it had been pretty amazing. I'd never felt anything quite like it. I flushed with sudden heat as a renewed surge of arousal made my pussy clench.

"You can take the toy out, honey," Henry called from the other side of the door. "I won't make you sleep with it."

Grinning wryly, I tossed it into the sink. He could deal with it.

"And don't forget to clean it up."

Shit. Letting out a breath, I took care of the chore and laid the toy on a clean hand towel to dry. I washed my hands and face, then contemplated the idea of another shower to buy myself some time. The door opened as I was considering my choices, and I turned to face him.

"You're stalling," Henry said quietly, tracing his hand down the leash dangling from the training collar I wore once upon an age ago.

He was right. I looked up into his soft brown eyes. It was totally unfair that he looked so effortlessly gorgeous. His beard was neatly trimmed, the edges following the line of his jaw. Cut short, it was more pepper than salt. The ragged pony tail was gone, revealing the soft waves of thick hair I used to love to touch. My hands twitched and I kept them forcibly at my sides.

"Why did you cut your hair?"

Smiling softly, he touched me, twisting a blue-dyed lock of my hair around one finger. "Same reason behind these blue and purple streaks, I imagine. I was ready for a change."

"And the suit?"

"Your show was black-tie." He crossed his arms over his ragged Pearl Jam T-shirt, then leaned a hip against the sink. "So, you sold the whole collection."

"Yeah." My cheeks heated and I looked away. "They all went to Patrick and Lexie from Stronghold."

"Maybe we should go for a visit."

I bit my lip and decided not to tell him I'd already thought about going. "Maybe," I finally said. "Were you serious about retiring?"

"Very serious. Since we're actually having an adult conversation, I'll make us some coffee." He touched my shoulder, gently pushing me to my knees, then led me across the basement to the small table. Leaving me on my cushion, he prepared our drinks. The Keurig whirred and groaned before spitting out the steaming brew. He swirled a few splashes of my favorite creamer into the cup, then brought it back and handed it to me.

"What happened?"

"Bethany," he replied, returning to the coffee maker. "She wanted to demote me to the production floor after I trained my replacement."

I winced, then took a sip from my cup. It was strangely comfortable to be like this. Me on my knees, naked. Him serving me. Me serving him. It was almost like old times—like there had never been distance between us.

This was a conversation we could have had on so many different occasions. He could have talked instead of shouting at me. I could have listened instead of tuning him out.

"I'm sorry."

"Don't be." Carrying his own cup, he sat down and laid a hand on my head, petting me like he used to. I resisted the urge to lean into his touch. "You were right about making changes, and it was time."

"I'm not sure I understand. You were devoted to that project."

He set his coffee down, then spread his knees, wordlessly asking me to move between them. When I did, he said, "I was, but it's nowhere near as important as you."

I had nothing to say in response and looked into my cup for inspiration. The smooth Kona brew refused to provide answers.

A callused finger stroked my jaw and he tipped my head up. "Tell me why you left. I know what was in your letter, but tell me why now."

"I don't have an answer you'll like," I muttered, leaning away from his touch.

His hand tightened around my jaw and he pulled me close. "Tell me your truths, Natalie. Look at me and tell me."

I stared helplessly into his fathomless brown eyes. "I didn't think you'd notice I was gone. I didn't think you'd even care. I waited until you went camping so I didn't have to…"

Biting my lip, I shook my head and sprang to my feet, then walked away. I needed distance. I couldn't let him touch me. If he did, I wasn't sure I'd be able to hold it together.

"Didn't have to…what?" he asked, his footsteps soft behind me. The heat of his body sent prickles down my spine and his soft breath wafted over my shoulder as he pulled me against his chest.

Tears welled in my eyes and I swallowed, my throat clogged. "I decided to wait until you were gone so I wouldn't have to see that I was right."

"Oh, Jesus, baby girl." He spun me around, then

wrapped me in a tight, crushing hug. "No, no, no."

His arms around me reminded me of things I'd wanted so badly to forget. Him holding me when I cried my heart out following our first unsuccessful IVF treatment. The incredibly intimate scenes we'd shared in this very basement. He'd brought me to tears then too, but those were tears of pleasure instead of loss and disappointment. The sobs I tried to hold back burst free.

CHAPTER SEVEN

Henry

I bit back a multitude of curses and swung Natalie into my arms, then carried her to the bondage bed. How could she have thought such things?

Maybe the better question would be why I'd allowed her to think them.

She cried as if her heart was breaking. My chest ached as I laid her down and crawled into bed next to her. I'd done this to her. To us. I crooned some nonsense words, cradling her against me, her tears soaking my T-shirt. "It's okay, honey," I whispered. "It's going to be fine."

Her breath hitched in her throat and she sat up, pulling away from me. "Where do we go now?" she asked softly.

"Come here," I ordered, refusing to allow her the distance. When she didn't immediately obey, I tugged her into my lap, sending up a short prayer of thanks she didn't resist. "Tell me your favorite memory of us. What's the one thing you remember from when we first started dating?"

Chuckling softly, she wiped at her eyes with a corner of the sheet. "Remember when we went to Myrtle Beach for spring break?"

"Yeah." I rested my chin on her head. "We were both broke, so we got space at a cheap campground and ate hot dogs without buns cooked on sticks over the fire."

"With mustard and ketchup packets from fast food places." She drew her knees up, resting her chin on crossed arms. "I miss that."

"The bugs too?"

She didn't look at me, but her lips twitched into a small smile. "Maybe not the bugs."

I petted her shoulders, her skin silky under my fingers. "We'd have breakfast at that little truck stop diner on route seventeen."

"All you could eat biscuits and gravy for three dollars."

"I remember going to Maine the first year we were married."

Laughing, she lifted her head. Her beautiful blue eyes sparkled with mirth. "We ate so much lobster, we both ended up sick."

"It was mostly the butter," I countered.

"I think I gained ten pounds on that trip."

"Me too." We fell into a comfortable silence. It was like things used to be between us, but I didn't believe for a minute all our problems would be solved over remembered vacations. I didn't think it was a mistake neither of us mentioned going to clubs.

"We haven't gone on a trip in ages," she murmured. To my delight, she stretched out and rested her head on my chest. I couldn't remember the last time I'd had Natalie's willing touch.

"If you could go anywhere—"

"Tahoe." A faint frown crossed her face and she turned to lay on her back.

"I remember." I pulled her into my arms again. "That little bed and breakfast with the playroom across the lake from the wedding chapel where we got married. Would you like to go back?"

"I don't know." She bit her lip, then looked up at

me. "Does it matter?"

"Yes." I tipped up her chin and kissed her. Natalie's lips met mine, teasing me with soft breathlessness. I swallowed a groan as my cock hardened. "It matters," I whispered against her mouth. "I want to make you happy again."

A tear dripped from the corner of her eye and I wiped it away. Making Natalie cry with pleasure or sensual desperation used to be one of my favorite pastimes, but her tears of sadness made my heart ache. "Can I get a do-over? I'm pretty sure we have another life left in this game."

Still crying, she choked out a laugh. "Yeah. A do-over."

Thank fuck. "I promise you won't regret it."

She nodded, then let out a sigh. "I guess we better clean up and go upstairs. Party's over."

"No, I said we're staying here."

Lifting her head, she stared at me in confusion. "But you said that was only until I agreed to come home. I need to get dressed and go to my apartment to pack."

"I said we were staying here until we got back to where we were," I corrected, kissing her silky shoulder. "We're not there yet."

"I'm not following." Natalie's eyes narrowed and she sat up, covering herself with the sheet.

I tugged the sheet from her, revealing her soft curves once more. "This is a do-over," I reminded her. "We're going to start from the beginning and restore the dynamic between us."

She laughed softly and shook her head. "Henry, do we need to do that? I mean, we're both on the wrong side of forty. You can't possibly expect me to trot around in a collar and chastity belt all day. And don't get me started on crawling like I used to. We'd have to install memory foam under all the carpets."

"Yes." I slipped a finger under her collar and pulled her close. "That's exactly what I expect. We'll work around the crawling."

Her eyes dilated and she shivered. "I—"

"Do you remember how wet it made you?" I trailed my lips across her jaw, feathering kisses under her ear. "Do you remember how it felt to kneel at the door for me, naked and needy? I remember ordering you to wait outside during the summer when the trees blocked the view from the road."

"Fuck." She breathed the word more than spoke it and her face flushed.

"Hands behind your head, your knees apart. You wore those black heels, your collar and chastity belt, but nothing else. Sometimes I'd park on the road and watch you twitch every time a car went by. You were so afraid someone would see, but exposing yourself on my order made you drip."

"I remember," she whispered, her eyes drifting shut.

She shifted her hips and pressed her thighs together. I wished I could see if she was wet. Actually, I wanted to push my head between her legs and taste it, but I was after a bigger prize. I would accept nothing less than her willing submission.

"Do you?" I asked, pulling back. She whimpered softly, but I wasn't about to give in. "Tell me what you'd do when you met me at the door."

Licking her lips, Natalie tried to turn away, but I held her still. "Tell me."

"I…" She swallowed and tried again. "You'd stop before you got to me, so I had to crawl. And then…"

"Then what?" I prompted.

"I'd kiss your shoes and ask for permission to suck your cock."

"Such a good girl." I petted her hair, brushing it out of her eyes. "I'd say yes, and you would look up at me while I fucked your pretty mouth. You never looked so beautiful until last night at your gallery show."

Her eyes shuttered and she drew her knees to her chest. "As I said, we're not in our twenties anymore. Aside from that, you're retired, and I still have to work on my next series. I just don't think—"

I kept my expression placid, but wanted to give her a little shake for being so stubborn. "That's right. Things have changed," I agreed. "We've changed. Does that mean we can't play anymore?"

Chewing on her lip, she shrugged and looked away. "I don't know."

Taking her hand, I pushed it between her legs, then let go. "Are you wet, Natalie? Did me reminding you of one of our daily rituals turn you on? Let me see."

Natalie

Christ, Henry's dom voice… I was like Pavlov's dog. Every time he got that raspy, gravel-over-silk tone, I obeyed. It didn't seem to matter that I'd left him, or that he'd scared the shit out of me with his fucked-up kidnapping stunt. He spoke, I dripped. It was a thing between us, and I couldn't stop it.

I didn't want to show him the slick moisture on my fingertips, but I couldn't lay there with my hand between my legs forever. There was too much temptation to ease the ache and touch my clit. The sadistic bastard knew it, and gave me a smirk.

"Are you afraid of what I might find?"

Fuck. Me. The ephemeral touch of his warm breath against my throat above the training collar sent another surge of heat into my core. I lifted my hand, curling my fingers into a fist.

"Yes, I'm wet, damn you."

"I bet you taste delicious." Gently, he pried my fist open, then drew my index finger into his mouth. My breath caught on another punch of arousal and he met my eyes, his tongue swirling to catch every drop of my juices.

"Henry, please…" I closed my eyes, unable to meet his knowing gaze. "I can't do this."

"Are you going to safeword before we've gotten started?" He leaned back against the pillows and tugged me securely against his chest. "I lied about that. You can safeword any time you want."

"Would you listen if I did?"

The flash of hurt in his eyes nearly made me take the words back. The one thing I knew without a doubt was Henry's absolute obedience to being safe, sane, and consensual. He'd cut off his own arm before he'd ignore a safeword. Well, aside from the whole kidnapping thing, but even then, he'd done absolutely nothing I'd have safeworded over.

"I deserved that," he murmured, kissing my temple. "I'm sorry."

"No, I shouldn't have said it."

"It's all right." His lips quirked into a wry smile. "I did make you think I pissed on you."

"I know." I chewed on my lip, then added, "But it was such a *you* thing to do."

"Oh?"

"Yeah. If I'd known it was you instead of some fuckwit kidnapper, I'd have trusted you weren't actually peeing on me."

Faster than I could blink, he had me turned over on my stomach, then a slap rang out like a rifle shot as he delivered a single punishing spank to my ass.

"Ouch! What was that for?"

In a soft voice full of warning, he said, "Language, little girl. You might recall how I broke you of dropping f-bombs before. That's going to be the first thing we work on."

"I don't think you can call me a little girl anymore," I retorted. "Remember us both being on the wrong side of forty?"

"Your ass still turns pink when I spank it." He rubbed my backside, then pushed his fingers between my legs.

When he brushed my clit, I drew in a shaky breath, desperate to control my surge of arousal. "All right, fine. Point taken."

Still stroking my sensitive flesh, he said, "Let's make a deal, baby. Stay down here with me for a week. Give me a chance to show you we can put our marriage back on track."

He pushed a finger inside me, making me clench around him. Damn him, he knew exactly how to hit all my buttons. My hips bucked and I bit back a groan. "Da...darn you. I can't think when you do that."

"I know. I don't want you to think. I want you to feel and remember how good it used to be." He added a second finger and my groan broke free. "We managed fifteen good years and a couple of bad ones, honey. I want to make the rest of them good for us, but I need you to meet me halfway."

Inside me, his fingers curled, tearing a ragged cry from my throat as he rubbed my g-spot. Wasn't this what I prayed for when I thought I was in the hands of a psychopath?

He pressed down on my clit with his thumb, sending agonizing pleasure rocketing through my core.

"Henry, please! Stop! I can't—"

"You have to say the right word if you truly want me to stop," he murmured, circling his thumb around my piercing as he pressed harder against the sweet spot inside me. "But if you come, I'll take that as agreement to my terms."

This... It was everything I'd been missing. With Henry, I always had choices. Always. Yet he was a demon, tempting and tantalizing me to sell my soul for the privilege of kneeling at his feet. His dominance was effortlessly, deliciously cruel and I wanted to give in. I didn't want to think anymore. I wanted so badly for him to carry the weight of us for awhile.

The force of my impending orgasm made me feel as if my insides were swelling, ballooning with the unspent force of a rising tempest. Breathing through my nose, I tried to tamp it down. I wasn't ready to take that step.

He sank his free hand into my hair and pulled my head up, the sting sending another pulse of need down my spine. "Let go, baby. I swear on my own life I will never give you reason to be sorry for your choice."

I screamed, letting the storm rage so powerfully it hurt. A flood of wetness soaked the bedding under me, my core clenching in one last agonizing spasm. Breathing hard, I tried to center my scattered thoughts as I shuddered under his soothing touch. Aftercare had always been one of Henry's favorite times. He used to spend hours at it, but I didn't know what would happen in this new dynamic of ours.

He stroked my sweaty hair away from my face and I leaned into his touch, my safeword balanced on the tip of my tongue. I swallowed it, grimacing at the taste. Maybe I should have used it, but it was too late. I truly didn't want to though. If there was a chance at getting back to where we used to be, I owed it to us both to take it.

"Ready. Player. One."

I let my head drop. There was no way I was going to let him see me laugh over his dumb game references. "Fuck you, Henry. Asparagus."

CHAPTER EIGHT

Henry

Her shoulders shook like she was trying to hold in a laugh. "You're safewording now?" I asked, hiding a smile.

"No game references," she snapped, lifting her head slightly to glare at me. "And if you say *finish herrr*, I'm walking out."

My laughter burst free and I covered her with a sheet, noting the goosebumps on her arms. "I'm going to get you a snack and some water," I said, climbing out of bed. "But I promise, no more game references. We'll discuss your language later."

She still shivered so I added a warm fleece blanket to the sheet covering her, then strode to the refrigerator. Cubes of cheese, olives, small tomatoes, and thin slices of cured salami and Parma ham went on a tray with a box of crackers. I even had small squares of her favorite chili-infused bittersweet chocolate.

"Oh, my God," she breathed, her eyes widening as I set the tray on the bed next to her. "You remembered everything."

"Almost. Your water is still in the fridge." I quickly retrieved a tumbler and the pitcher, already filled with cucumber and lime slices floating in the iced water. Returning, I filled the glass, then settled behind her and helped her lean back against my chest.

When she reached for the water, I said, "Ah ah.

That isn't how aftercare works."

"I remember," she said softly, clasping her hands together in her lap.

"You don't have to remember everything. In fact, I don't want you to." I held the straw for her, letting her drink her fill. "We're going to make some new memories, but some things aren't going to change."

"Like what?"

"Aftercare. That's my job, and you're not to do a thing except take it." I put a cube of cheese to her lips, letting her take it from my fingers.

"You got all my favorite snacks." She opened her mouth for the piece of ham I held, then added, "How long have you been planning this? It must have been weeks, but how did you know about my gallery show?"

And just like that, Natalie's brilliant intellect was back online. It might take a few hours for her body to shake off the effects of a scene, but her brain always went full steam ahead. Grabbing my phone, I pulled up my aftercare playlist and sent it to the Bluetooth speakers. Hopefully, the calming strings and soft vocals would give her mind something to chew on.

I wish I'd remembered the lavender-scented wax melts, but I hadn't been thinking too clearly when I plotted my kidnapping. Still, my efforts were as good as two-day express delivery could make them. I even had her favorite wine to go with supper later. God bless meal services.

Hell, now that I was retired, maybe I'd learn to cook. I could grill a mean steak at least.

"Natalie, we'll talk about this later after supper."

"But how—"

I slipped an olive between her lips, silencing her question. "Later," I repeated firmly. "After we eat supper."

She swallowed and relaxed, her body softening in my arms. "Yes, sir."

"Good girl." Although I was disappointed she didn't call me Master, I'd take what I could get for now. I kissed the top of her head, inhaling the sweet scent of her hair. "I promise, we'll talk tonight."

I kept feeding her, supremely content to hold her. I couldn't remember the last time I'd taken such pleasure in simply caring for my wife. It was aftercare—something I'd done hundreds of times for her—yet it seemed different somehow. Maybe it was the reconnection after spending so long drifting apart.

She sucked the last of the grape tomatoes from my fingers and let out a sigh. "Thanks," she whispered. "That was delicious."

"Do you want more?"

"No, I'm full."

"All right." I helped her sit up, then eased out from behind her. "Lie down and rest for a few hours."

She shook her head and tugged the blanket over her shoulders. "Henry, we need to talk about your kidnapping game. I need to know what—"

"Natalie, you can either nap in bed with me, or in your cage with a penis gag. Which will it be?"

Eyes wide, she shook her head and drew a finger across her lips. I hardened at the thought of silencing her as I used to—with my dick in her mouth. It was too soon, but her immediate obedience sent a thrill of hope through me.

"Good girl," I murmured, helping her lie down. "Rest for an hour or so, then I have a surprise for you."

"What is it?" Her back to me, she curled up and

let me be the big spoon, her hands tucked under her chin.

God, I'd missed this. Just having her in my arms again was everything to me. I didn't need anything else. Clearing my throat, I said, "It wouldn't be a surprise if I told you."

"Hmm. What about my punishment for swearing?"

"Later."

"Ugh! Henry, you—"

"Careful, sweetheart," I warned. "You don't want to add to it, do you?"

She huffed out a cute little breath. If she'd been standing, I was sure there would have been a foot stomp involved. "You know I hate having punishments hanging over me."

"Yep, I know."

"F… Sadist."

"Go to sleep before I reconsider that penis gag."

Natalie

It felt good to have Henry spooning me. His scent wasn't what I was used to, but everything else was the same and it was…right. I used to love listening to the sound of his breathing as he fell asleep. Smiling softly, I shifted in his arms to quiet his snores.

Just like old times.

Although I was warm, comfortable, and content, my mind spun, chewing over how much time we'd wasted. How had we grown so far apart? Our failure to have a child had been a catalyst, but we shouldn't have let it drive us away from each other. Yet maybe we needed those dark times.

One of us had needed to upset the applecart, so to speak. And he was right. We had to go back before we moved forward. The dynamic we had before wouldn't work for us now. I no longer had a fixed schedule. I worked when the muse struck and considering we'd be living off my earnings from my art, I had to keep producing. Well, unless he found something else to occupy his time. I didn't see him being idle for long, but I had no idea what he might want to do.

Five years ago, I would have known. We used to tell each other everything. Speaking of which, I needed to set up an appointment with my therapist and ask what she thought about the situation with Henry.

The trust that used to come to us so easily was gone. Oh, I still trusted him not to hurt me. That would never be in question. He was king of the predicament, emperor of tantalizing agony, and the absolute ruler of my body. He used to be the ruler of my heart too, but I was beginning to think we could get that back.

I couldn't be sorry for my decision to leave, and I wasn't angry about Henry's harebrained scheme to kidnap me. Okay, maybe I was still a little irritated about the faux watersports, but I'd get over it. We'd also need to delete that video. I trusted Henry would keep it secure, but there was no reason to save it. He'd already made his point.

Closing my eyes, I let myself doze in his arms, the soft elevator music he liked to play for aftercare still running in the background. He had a damned playlist for everything. To him, music was part of the scene, as were certain fragrances at different times. I let my lips twist into a smirk. He'd forgotten the lavender.

He'd always planned scenes so meticulously.

That one missing item, while insignificant, was an important insight into his thoughts. It made him... fallible, and I liked it.

"You're not sleeping," he whispered in my ear, startling me. "Is there something you want to tell me?"

I swallowed hard. That statement used to mean he knew I wasn't telling him everything. It said, *tell me your truths before I have to make you*.

"I couldn't sleep," I said, deciding honesty would be my safest option. "Just thinking about things, I guess." Rolling over, I faced him. "Enjoying spooning with you. I missed that."

"Me too." Cupping my jaw, he kissed me slowly, lingering to brush my lower lip with the tip of his tongue.

To distract myself from the welling tremor of arousal, I asked, "I'm curious about something. Why did you drive straight home after your trip? You usually stop near Toledo for the night."

Cheeks reddening over his beard, he gave me a shamefaced grin. "You have to promise not to laugh."

I drew an X over my chest, wondering what would make him react so uncharacteristically to an honest question. "Cross my heart."

"It's the Dad Bod Dom challenge."

"The... Excuse me?"

"Yeah. Sounds dumb, doesn't it?" He rolled to his back, but kept me tucked against his side. "We started talking, and figured out you and I weren't the only ones having problems. It was Logan's idea, but we all agreed to it. Ray decided to join a gym."

"I see." Although it was comforting to know Henry and I weren't the only ones with issues, I was stupidly hurt to learn he'd aired our dirty laundry.

"What did you tell them?"

"I didn't think it was anyone's business, and just said we were both too busy to talk like we used to. Aside from that, I wasn't about to discuss our issues with three men who desperately need to take their wives for a weekend away from their kids."

I nodded, glad he hadn't overshared. Henry made a good point about that as well. In my desire for a child, I'd lost sight of how a baby would have impacted our relationship. "And Leyla has an infant," I murmured. "It must be especially hard for her, considering her…you know."

"Yeah." His arm tightened around me and he kissed my temple. "Faris wasn't in the best of moods. Anyway, since we're both awake, let's go see your surprise."

"All right," I slid out of bed, trying to control my burgeoning excitement mixed with trepidation when he handed me my tennis shoes, then pulled on jeans and a T-shirt. "Where are we going?"

"You'll see."

"We can't go anywhere. You shredded my clothes."

The skin under his eyes crinkled into a grin. "Put your shoes on, pet."

"Oh f…" I peeked up at him and shut my mouth, then did as he asked. "Henry, I—"

"Shh." He pushed his hand under my hair and cradled the back of my neck, making me nearly melt into a puddle at his feet. "Give me your trust, Natalie. I won't abuse it, I promise."

"I…" Nodding, I let out a breath. "Okay."

"There's my good girl," he crooned. "But one more thing." Reaching into his pocket, he pulled out a long chain with a delicate clip on one end, then snapped it on my clit ring.

The extra weight pulled the ring down, and I nearly cried out at the fierce need surging through my core. "Oh, God."

I was going to fucking die. No, I was going to kill him. He tugged on the chain and I stumbled forward. "Henry, please. I can't."

"Thanks for the reminder. You can't go outside without a plug, right?" He led me to the bed and pressed down on my shoulders, making me bend over, then nudged my feet apart. "Do you think I should use the ginger again? I bought a couple of pounds. It would be a shame to waste it."

Fuck. I kept the word inside, thank goodness, but he was moving too fast. We hadn't scened in years, and I wasn't ready for the immediate immersion into his sadistic games. Maybe I needed more aftercare from this morning. Or that nap I didn't get. Something. Hell, I didn't know what I needed.

"Yellow, please."

The next thing I knew, the chain was gone and he had me curled in his lap on the bed. "It's okay, sweetie. I went too fast, and we aren't ready."

"No, I—"

"We're good," he interrupted, letting me rest against his chest. "We're going to be just fine. I'm so glad you told me."

"I'm sorry." Tears pricked at my eyes, and I felt like I'd disappointed him. No, it was more that I disappointed myself.

He gave me a tight hug, then tapped my nose. "Never be sorry for using a safeword, Natalie. You know better."

"I... Okay." I took a deep breath and sat up. "I'm okay."

"Good." He cocked his head, then shifted me to the bed to pull off his T-shirt, revealing his chest dusted with silver and black hair. "Put this on," he said, handing it to me. "We'll skip the chain and the plug."

"I'm okay with the chain," I whispered, pulling the shirt over my head.

A wide, delighted smile lit his features and I had to return it as he clipped the shining metal to my clit ring. "Oh, Natalie, I'm so proud of you."

The weight of the chain seemed different somehow. It still pulled, making wetness trickle down my thigh, yet it was a connection instead of a leash—a way for him to give me the tease of pleasure without actually touching me.

He led me upstairs and out the French doors leading to the deck off the kitchen, then down the few steps to the back yard. We had part of it fenced off with tall privacy panels and we had no close neighbors, so I didn't worry about anyone seeing.

Aside from my rosebushes, spent now but for a few late-blooming varieties, the only thing back here was an old pole barn. We'd entertained the idea of turning it into a guest house, but it became one of those projects that got pushed down the honey-do list. As far as I knew, it was still empty.

"Where are we going?" I asked, stepping carefully behind him. The chain swung and brushed teasingly between my legs. I was so damned wet, my thighs slid against each other as I walked.

"You'll see."

CHAPTER NINE

Henry

I wanted to hurry her along, but I kept myself to a slow pace. I wasn't about to risk her stumbling with the chain attached to her clit piercing. I couldn't wait to show her what I envisioned. It had been an afterthought—something that occurred to me only today.

Would it please her? God, I hoped so. Maybe I should have waited until I had time to finish what I wanted. Then again, I'd need her input to make it right.

"We're here," I said, pointing at the old barn near the fence.

Lines of confusion marred her pretty face. "I don't understand. What's going on?"

"Welcome to your new studio."

"My... What are you talking about?"

I slid the door up, then led her inside. The place was empty but for some cobwebs, our riding mower, and an old freestanding cast iron stove set in the middle. "I'm thinking I'll replace that garage door with French doors. They face east, so you'll have plenty of natural light. I can replace the rest of the windows with larger ones and cut a few trees down. We can add some skylights too."

"Holy...sugar," she whispered. "Henry, are you serious? Why?"

My face warmed and I had to force myself to

meet her questioning gaze. "Partly because it's been standing here for years waiting for us to do something with it, but mostly because you deserve it. It's also kind of a lame apology for kidnapping you."

A wry grin teased the corners of her mouth. "You scared the crap out of me, but I forgive you." She turned away and gazed up into the rafters. "Are you sure we can do this?"

"Sure. I'm retired, so I have plenty of time to do the work. Besides, if you're planning to build bondage furniture, you'll need tools you probably don't want in the house. We'll put in a bathroom and a daybed so you can take a snooze if you need to. Maybe a kitchenette too, and we can add a deck off the back if you want to work outside."

I unclipped the chain, but she didn't notice. Turning in a circle, she scanned the space, her lips parted in astonishment. Barely a second later, I had an armful of woman launch herself at me and wrap her legs around my waist.

"This is so amazing. I would have never thought of it."

She lowered her head and kissed me as I was trying to catch my balance, and I counted myself lucky we didn't go sprawling. Not sexy at all. But damn, her kisses made me want to press her against the wall and fuck her silly.

When she came up for air, I chuckled softly. "I take it you like the idea?"

Her eyes glistened with moisture and she gave me a brilliant grin. "I love it. Thank you."

"You're welcome." I led her outside and shut the overhead door behind us. "If you're interested in a partner, I got an A in high school wood shop. You design the furniture and I'll build it."

"I…" She smiled again, then reached up to kiss my cheek. "I'd like that very much."

I couldn't believe my surprise had gone over so well. I'd been half afraid she'd want to keep a studio elsewhere. I wouldn't have stopped her, but I wanted to be the one meeting her needs. The idea of building her furniture had been an afterthought, but the more I considered the idea, the better I liked it. The challenge, plus the opportunity to create something with her, excited me.

Hell, maybe it could be my new side hustle. I'd always liked working with my hands, and I used to be pretty good with a router. There could be handmade paddles, intricate St. Andrew's crosses, benches…

"I'm glad, honey." I took her hand and led her back to the house. "We'll get your punishment for swearing out of the way, then have supper."

Letting out a sigh, she lowered her head and trudged inside. "I'm trying," she muttered, making her way to the basement door.

I followed her down the stairs. "I know, and you're doing very well. We're going to take it one step at a time, so all you have to think about for the next few days is losing the f-bombs."

"There's going to be more than that," she countered.

"Yes, but for now, that's your only rule. The rest will be play and experimentation to see what works for us and what doesn't."

She chewed on her lip for a few seconds, then nodded. "Okay. Sounds like a plan."

"I'm glad you think so. Now, be a good girl and strip for me, please."

"Yes, m…sir."

She toed off her shoes and socks, then pulled the

T-shirt over her head. She'd almost called me Master and I resisted the urge to pump my fist in triumph.

"Thank you. Get the Delrin from the rack, then stand by the spanking bench and present it. You don't have to kneel like you used to. We'll skip that part until we get carpet installed."

Intending to pull up music for a scene, I reached in my pocket for my phone, then remembered this was a punishment. I had to get myself into the right headspace. It might be planned in just as much detail, but it wasn't something either of us would enjoy. Correction was hard and fast, but we considered the matter closed once it was over.

I centered my thoughts on her, what I was about to do, and my responsibility. I made a promise to her and to myself. She had to trust I would be there for her, and that I'd do what I said without judgment or anger.

When she reached her position next to the bench, I strode to her and took the cane from her outstretched hands. "Good girl. Do you remember what happens next?"

She cut her eyes toward the bench, then let out a breath and turned to face it. "I remember."

Natalie

The familiar padded leather was cold and I shivered as I laid myself over it. The act was muscle memory—something I'd done hundreds of times over the years.

Some things never changed. I still got the itch of heated trepidation the minute my stomach touched the bench and my fingers slid into the worn grooves on the bottom bolster where I'd gripped them so many times before. My knees found the thickly cushioned rests, spreading my thighs apart.

I inhaled the scent of the glycerin soap Henry always used to clean his leather. It was like finding a seat in a worn, but familiar easy chair after a long journey.

"How many do you think I should give you?"

"It will be as many as you think I need, m...sir." The honorific he wanted almost spilled out. Again. I didn't want to laugh about it anymore, but it was a step I wasn't sure I was ready to take.

"You remember," he said, his dom voice like a brush of watered silk down my spine.

"Yes, m...sir."

Henry's body heat smothered me as he leaned over and touched his lips to the back of my neck. "You aren't going to say it, even though part of you wants to."

He straightened and I shivered at the absence of his warmth, but didn't answer. The top cushion pressed into my belly, a reminder of what was to come.

"If you say it and truly mean it, I won't punish you for swearing," he breathed into my ear. "Just say it one time, Natalie."

Why was this so hard? Henry was my Master whether I used the word or not. He always had been, but maybe I needed to take that step toward him. Maybe he needed that affirmation of commitment between us.

I blinked back a few tears, then closed my eyes. "Master."

The cane clattered across the floor and he knelt in front of me. He cupped my cheeks in his callused hands and kissed me, a sweet brush of his lips against mine that made tears well in my eyes again.

He cleared his throat, then rested his forehead against mine. "Thank you, baby girl. I love you so damned much, and I'm going to live up to that word, I promise."

"I love you too," I whispered, opening my eyes.

Suspicious wetness glistened on his cheeks and he kissed me again. Straightening, he put his hands on my shoulders to help me up. "Let's go upstairs. You can wear one of my T-shirts and a pair of sweats until we can get your clothes."

I almost got up, then tightened my fingers around the hand grips. "No, Master. I… You promised we'd stay down here for a week."

"I want to sleep with you in our marriage bed, honey. We don't need to—"

"Yes, we do," I whispered. "You said we needed the time to rediscover each other."

Indecision creased his brow for a few seconds before his face relaxed into a smile. "We'll spend the days down here, but we'll sleep in our own bed."

"Look at us, negotiating like grownups." Laughing, he slapped my ass, reminding me why I was bent over our spanking bench. "Will you do my punishment now, Master?"

"No." He tried to pull me up, but I refused to let go. "I said I would waive it if you called me Master."

"You also said not swearing was the only thing I had to focus on this week."

His face clouded, but he nodded and picked up the cane. "You're not the only one who needs to remember how things worked best for us. You've never been able to move forward unless we got a punishment done and out of the way."

"Yes, Master. It will be as many as you think I need," I said, repeating the expected response.

"Five. You'll count them, please."

He palmed my ass and rubbed briskly. Unlike a regular play scene, that was all the warmup I'd get. The cane whistled and I gasped as the first line of fire lit up the top of my ass.

"One." Henry was an expert with the cane. The second lash fell, exactly where he wanted it. I let go of the pain caused by our infertility.

"Two." If I looked in the mirror, there would be exactly three centimeters between marks. He was nothing if not precise. The dissatisfaction from a twenty-year teaching career vanished.

"Three!" I hissed out a pained breath from the sting. The lines across my ass throbbed in time with my heartbeat and my anger at his kidnapping melted away.

"F...four." Tears pricked my eyes. Swallowing a sob, I tightened my grip on the bolster. My rage at his distance and lack of communication flowed out.

"One more, baby girl," he murmured, tracing one of the blossoming welts with the tip of the cane. I shuddered at the itch of swelling flesh. The last one would be the hardest and he would lay it across the tender skin where my butt met my thighs. I tightened my muscles, even though I knew I shouldn't.

"Yes, Master." The words were a choked whisper, but the act of breathing made my tension disappear. Before I could take another breath, the cane whistled again. A streak of flame lit up my ass from his last stroke and I screamed, my body seizing with the pain.

"Natalie, count it or we have to start over," he warned.

"Five!" I collapsed in a boneless mess against the bench, my hands falling away from the grips as I sobbed out cathartic tears. Those five cane strokes weren't just punishment for a few f-bombs. They were punishment for everything, and I let go of all the self-pity and blame I'd heaped on myself for years.

Henry stroked my shoulders and back, his firm touch soothing. He wouldn't rub my ass to ease the sting. It was part of the punishment, as was what would come next. My knees wobbled, but I managed to get up and stand without help.

I hugged him, resting my face against the crisp hair on his chest. "Thank you for my punishment, Master." Letting go, I turned and walked to my corner, then folded my arms behind my back, my hands on my elbows.

He touched my shoulder, then kissed my cheek, his beard soft against my skin. "You don't need corner time, baby. It's okay. We're done now, and the misbehavior is gone."

Shaking my head, I widened my stance and rested my forehead against the wall. The position pushed my butt out. Henry liked to see the results of his work.

His sigh feathered across the back of my neck and he kissed me again. "Ten minutes, baby girl, then we'll put some arnica on your stripes."

Perfect.

CHAPTER TEN

Henry

I set a timer on my phone, then grabbed the pitcher of water from the fridge and poured two glasses. Natalie would need hydrating once she finished her corner time. Hell, I could use something a little stronger, but I intended to limit myself to one glass of wine with supper. My alcohol abuse hadn't done us any favors and I needed to be better.

Master. She used the title without giggling, and most importantly, without being forced. I never thought I'd hear it from her. Taking a sip of water, I leaned against the counter and watched her. God, she was beautiful.

Her hair was a sex-tangled mess flowing over her shoulders. Long and lean after a lifetime of jogging, her body was every bit as gorgeous as the day I married her. Yet her physical beauty wasn't the important thing. It wasn't why I loved her.

Natalie was my other half, and a piece of my soul I hadn't realized was missing until she left me. I needed it back more than I needed to breathe.

What was going on in her head? She used to share every thought with me, but the distance between us made her retreat behind an icy shell of indifference. I wasn't blaming her though. I bore just as much responsibility for it as she did.

More than she did, I admitted to myself. I was the Master, and I should have known better after so many years together. I glanced down at the timer, wishing it would move faster. I might not be the one with stripes across my backside, but the punishment was as much for me as it was for her. I didn't like punishing Natalie. It always made me feel like I'd failed her, and the corner time was my penance.

Instead of the aftercare I was desperate to do, I had to wait. I couldn't touch her, wipe her tears, or tend her until that damned clock ticked down. When the numbers on my phone showed only a few seconds remaining, I turned it off and went to her.

"Time's up, sweetheart," I murmured, easing her hands from her elbows. When her arms dropped, I helped her into the bathroom and dampened a washcloth with cold water. Kneeling behind her, I pressed the cloth against her bottom, making sure none of the cane strokes had broken her skin. I never had, but accidents happened. There was no such thing as being too careful with a cane.

Her shoulders dropped and she let out a breath. "Thanks. That feels good."

"You're welcome." I grabbed the arnica gel and dabbed it on the welts. "How are you feeling?"

Giggling softly, she said, "My butt hurts."

I smiled and swatted her bottom, carefully avoiding the cane marks. "Smartass. What's going on in your head, honey?"

She was silent for several seconds while I continued my task. As I was about to prompt her again, she finally spoke. "I feel…good. Really good."

"How so?" I checked her backside one more time to make sure I hadn't missed any spots, then led her to the couch and sat next to her.

"I know the cane was supposed to be for swearing, but…" She turned to look at me, her blue eyes pensive. "I don't know. It's weird."

I laid a fleece blanket over her, then wrapped an arm around her. "I'm not going to judge anything you tell me."

"Yeah, I know. I'm just…" She laughed softly and rested her head on my chest. "It was almost like every stroke was me letting go of something hurtful to us."

"Like what?"

"Infertility, twenty years in a job I hated." She paused, then added, "Us giving up on each other for so long. It's like all that s…stuff lost the power to hurt us."

Giving her a squeeze, I kissed her forehead. "You can swear, just not the f-bombs."

"No, it's okay. It won't hurt me to give it up." She peered up at me, then added, "Sort of like you giving up booze. I haven't seen you drink all day."

"I was crazy hung over when I quit my job."

"I went out with Charles and drank my weight in martinis on the last day of school."

Resisting the urge to tighten my fingers on her delicate jaw, I lifted her chin. "Who's Charles?"

She blinked in surprise. "Charles Benson, the owner of the gallery where I had my show. He probably introduced himself to you."

My cheeks heated and I loosened my grip on her chin. "Yeah, sorry. I got incredibly, unreasonably jealous there for a second. He did introduce himself."

Giggling, she shook her head. "He'll be tickled to know that."

I grunted, secretly pleased my stupidity made her laugh. "Where did that dress come from? I'm hoping you'll wear it again for me, but not in public."

"The dress wasn't mine. I borrowed it from Eric."

I arched a brow and she laughed again.

"Eric is a drag queen by the name of Erica Gardot. Charles goes by Chloe. They grouped up and turned this middle-aged Cinderella into a princess for a few hours."

"Hey." I tugged her hair, forcing her to look at me. "You're my princess. Always have been, always will be."

Her eyes darkened and she licked her lips. Reaching up, she wrapped her hand around the back of my neck and kissed me. I groaned and pulled her into my lap, and she twisted in my arms until she straddled my thighs. Knowing her core was open and waiting just above me nearly made my dick burst through my zipper. She whimpered and ground her pussy against me.

"God, Natalie." I caught her lips again, deepening our kiss, then nearly choked when her little hands went to my waist and unbuttoned my jeans.

"I want you to make love to me," she breathed. "Please, Master."

There was no way I was going to refuse her. I had a scant few seconds to wonder if I should set up a scene before she wrapped a hand around my cock and positioned me at the entrance to her body.

Her warm heat surrounded me, sucking me in as she lowered herself and rocked her hips. I let the sensation of her wash over me. How had I forgotten how wonderful it was to make love to my wife?

We didn't need a scene. All we needed was each other. I surged into her, meeting her thrusts with my own as I pulled her in for another kiss. Scorching hot, she consumed me, fanning the flames between us with her knowing touch.

"Sit up, baby. Let me see those beautiful tits."

When she obeyed, I took a few seconds to just look at her. Face flushed, she threw her head back and moaned while her hips rocked. Ripe and full, her breasts were lush handfuls and I cupped them, teasing her nipples with my thumbs. Jerking, she cried out and her channel spasmed around me.

"God, Henry!"

"I remember how sensitive your pretty nipples are," I said, pinching them. "I used to love to see you come just from me sucking them. Maybe I'll do that later."

"Fuck... Please..."

Her guttural begging almost made me come. I closed my eyes, forcing it back. We'd have to alter her no swearing rule. Hearing the profane word in her sex voice...

Then again... "Oh, baby girl. There might be another punishment in your future for swearing," I whispered. "I'll put you on the cross with a clamp on your clit and use a flogger on your sweet tits until you come from it."

Screaming, she arched her back as her inner walls clamped down on me, rippling with the force of her orgasm. Christ, watching her climax was something I'd never tire of seeing. I wanted to give her another, but there was no way I was going to last. It had been too long. In a desperate attempt to get a few more seconds before I exploded, I pulled back and held my breath.

Natalie swirled her hips, making me bite back a curse. "Fuck me like you mean it, Henry."

"Oh, naughty girl." I grinned, letting her see teeth. "You're in for it now." Easing her off my lap, I stood and pulled her to her feet, then led her back to the spanking bench.

"I have been naughty, haven't I?" Her voice was soft and husky from crying out her passion and I loved it.

"Very, very naughty." I pushed her shoulders down, encouraging her onto the bench, then grabbed the vibrating wand from the toy chest. "You definitely need a punishment."

Her giggles cut off the minute she saw what was in my hand, and her eyes widened as I locked it into place under her. I hadn't intended to, but I also grabbed lube and let it dribble down the crack of her backside, working it into her asshole.

"Naughty girls get fucked in the ass, don't they, baby?"

Oh, God."

Natalie

This was what had been missing from our relationship for too many years. Play. A sense of fun and exploration. The sex was awesome, and my insides still quivered—especially when I knew the vibrating wand positioned under my clit would sing the song of its people any second.

Enjoying each other because we could and we wanted to. No deadlines, no thoughts of work… No goddamned ovulation charts. I had no idea how much I needed this.

"Tell me a color, baby girl," Henry said softly, leaning down to whisper in my ear. He stroked my shoulders, easing tense muscles into languorous relaxation.

"Green as grass, Master." I smiled at the pleased grin on his face, but felt no urge to giggle like I usually did.

"Good girl." He was only mostly successful at

replacing the happy expression with what he probably hoped was a stern glare. "Tell me why you're being punished," he ordered.

"I'm being punished because I asked you to fuck me like you meant it."

"Very good, so—"

"Are you going to fuck me like you mean it, Master?"

His face turned red and he choked out a laugh. "I love you so damned much, Natalie."

Kneeling, he kissed me, and I screeched into his mouth when he turned on the vibe. It went zero to sixty in no seconds flat. I clenched my fists around the bolster, desperate to hang on as he eased more lube into my asshole.

"Oh, my God," I breathed. My hips bucked and I let out a sharp cry when he slapped my ass right over the welts from the cane. It stung, but sent warmth deep into my core as he worked two fingers into me, readying me for him.

"Feel good?"

"Yes, so good." I twitched again, desperate to grind my pussy against the buzzing toy.

"Good." He eased his thick cock into my back channel, moving gently until his hips bumped against my ass. The ring in the crown of his cock brushed against my sensitive tissues, making me bite back a groan. "Do. Not. Come."

"No, please!" I begged. He pushed into me until all I could feel was the slick glide of his penetration against the maddening tease of the vibe.

"Pleading for mercy won't stop this punishment, baby, but you know what to say if it's too much." He thrust harder, nearly making me lose my damned mind, then set up a rhythm he knew would send me over.

Henry didn't have to worry about me safewording. That was the last thing on my mind. All I could think about was breathing and keeping the massive orgasm stalled somewhere between my navel and pussy. But it was there, and swirled in my belly like a whirlpool of lava.

"You feel so good around my cock, baby. How long do you think I can hold us on the edge? Ten minutes? Maybe twenty?"

He leaned down and bit my shoulder, sinking a fist into my hair. "What do you think? Can I edge us for twenty minutes?"

I cried out, desperate to hold back as my pulse pounded in time with his thrusts. "Henry, please! I can't—"

"Count with me, Natalie," he gritted out, his voice hoarse and breathless. "We'll go on one."

"Three…"

I matched my voice to his, saying the number with him. Soon. I was going to die the proverbial little death. I'd be lucky if my heart didn't stop.

"Two…"

Closing my eyes, I took a deep breath, my entire body clenching in preparation.

"One."

Shouting, he thrust into me one last time and I screamed out my release, my body quaking with aftershocks of the best fucking orgasm I'd ever had. Collapsing to my back, Henry's breaths sounded like he'd run a marathon.

Me? I just felt boneless and supremely content. I'd be happy to sleep here on this spanking bench all night, with him keeping me warm. Fortunately, Henry had a little more mental focus than I did. He turned off the vibe and pulled out, letting a stream of liquid trickle down my leg.

"Let's get you in the shower," he murmured, helping me off the bench and into the bathroom.

My knees felt like pudding, too soft and squishy to hold my weight. I staggered into the shower, propping myself in a corner until Henry could help me stand. He washed me carefully, and though it was sensual and pleasurable, it wasn't sexual. I was pretty much done, and could only muster a faint twinge of interest in my lady bits while he cleaned me up.

I wished I'd taken that nap earlier, but it might not have helped. Henry Mercer officially rocked my world. I couldn't even call it a scene. It was unscripted, unplanned, and probably the most profound sexual experience of our lives.

I felt closer to him than ever before. Like the distance between us was gone, and there was nothing left for us but to move forward into our shared future. It might not include the children I'd always wanted, but it was ours and it would be amazing.

"Give me a color, sweetheart," he said softly, rinsing shampoo from my hair.

"I'm green, Master. And I love you very much."

"Me too. I'm so glad you're home."

To my utter and everlasting disgust, I burst into tears. Damned perimenopause. Guaranteed to make a smart woman stupid faster than Chris Hemsworth's abs.

CHAPTER ELEVEN

Henry

Natalie's tears made my chest ache. It was a physical pain like no other and I wanted to run as far and as fast as I could just to get away from it. But I couldn't. She was crying because of me, and I'd sooner die than let her down again.

Scooping her into my arms, I carried her back to the couch. We were dripping wet, but I didn't give a shit. Pulling the blanket across the seat, I sat down, cuddling her in my lap.

"Baby, when you're ready, you need to tell me what's wrong," I said softly. "Did I hurt you?"

She sniffed, an indelicate sound that made me hide a smile, then said, "I feel absolutely amazing. That was the best sex ever, and I couldn't ask for a more perfect partner."

"Then…" I cast about for something to say. "Why the hell are you crying?"

Laughing through her tears, she shook her head. "I have no idea. Isn't that the dumbest thing you've ever heard?"

"Sugar drop?" Using a corner of the blanket, I wiped her face. I'd have to get a few towels sooner or later, and we'd need to clean up our toys, but all that could wait.

"Maybe." Her eyes twinkled. "Do you remember what your mom used to say about emotional old women?"

"Ugh." I lowered my face into her hair and shuddered. "Nope. I blocked that out on the advice of, you know, everyone. Besides, you're not old."

In a remarkable impression of my mother, she said, "You better get yourself pregnant before you hit—"

"...*The Change*," we finished together. "Patent pending."

Natalie's laughter faded and she laid her head on my chest. "She meant well."

"Yeah, but I'm sorry for all the times she made you feel like a failure. You're not."

"She wasn't so bad. I mean, I get it. She really wanted grandkids, and you're an only child. At least I have nieces and nephews to keep my parents occupied."

"True." I tugged her hair to make her look at me. "Are you sure you're okay?"

"Yes, I'm sure." She kissed me, a quick brush of her lips against mine. "I'm going to dry off and try to do something with my hair. Maybe we can watch a movie later."

"And figure out what's for supper. I have a bunch of frozen stuff from one of those online meal services."

"Nice. What's on the menu?" Her bare feet left wet footprints on the concrete. I'd really have to get carpet installed down here—especially for the winter.

I found my phone and pulled up the order. "Chicken Marsala, steak Diane, salmon Florentine, pad Thai—"

"I'll take that. Are there egg rolls?"

"No, sorry, but I can order some if you want. It only takes a few..." I jumped to my feet and raced up the stairs. I knew exactly what we were having for supper.

"Where are you going?" She came out of the bathroom, a towel wrapped around her as she pulled a comb through her hair.

"Be right back!"

I raced upstairs and skidded on the kitchen floor, nearly wiping out against the refrigerator as I yanked open the freezer. "Where is it? C'mon, I know we had some."

I dug deeper, past the ice cream, a bottle of vodka, and some frozen vegetables that probably needed to be tossed. Finally finding my prize, I lifted it over my head in triumph. "Yes!"

"What on earth are you doing, Henry?" Natalie asked from the top of the stairs.

"One sec," I replied, my head stuffed in the cupboard. I found what I needed, then dug in the utensil drawer for the last few things and laid everything for Natalie's perfect meal on the counter. "Okay, come see what we're having for supper."

She padded across the kitchen, her brow wrinkled with confusion. When she saw what I had, her eyes filled with tears again and she covered her mouth with one trembling hand. "Just like Myrtle Beach," she whispered.

"I'll zip a few sleeping bags together and we'll sleep under the stars tonight. So, what do you think?"

Her eyes fixed on the hot dogs, she nodded, then gave me a brilliant smile. "Perfect, and I might even have something for dessert."

"There's your favorite ice cream."

"Nope," she replied pointing at the top shelf in the cupboard. "Marshmallows, graham crackers—"

"S'mores," I finished, reaching up for her prizes, along with an unopened package of chocolate bars.

"And we have sticks we didn't have to pick up off the ground," she said, pointing at the skewers. "But we might have some campfire forks in the garage. I'm pretty sure we kept them when we moved here."

"I know where they are. Be right back!"

"Henry, wait!"

Her laughter followed me out and I rummaged through our old camping gear. "I knew you were in here," I murmured, pulling two long forks and a couple of pie irons from the pile, along with sleeping bags. We might not be on the beach, but I could recreate everything else from our first vacation together.

"I have everything we need," I pronounced, hauling my finds inside. "And these." I held up the pie irons. "Think we have some pie filling somewhere?"

Everything was going to be perfect. I couldn't think of a better way to start our new life together—especially when it put a brilliant smile on my wife's face. Maybe the guys had the right idea. Dad Bod Doms, for the win.

Natalie

How had Henry known the exact thing to make me truly believe we'd work things out? God, I wished I'd upset our marital applecart years ago. There had been too much wasted time.

While he was carrying stuff outside, I went upstairs and rummaged for a pair of his sweats and a T-shirt, along with clean socks. If it wasn't too chilly to be outside naked, the bugs would eat us alive.

Then again, maybe I needed to get my head back in the D/s game. I had to put in the effort to meet him halfway. Instead of dressing, I carried the clothes downstairs, along with fresh stuff for Henry. Even if he didn't let me wear anything, I had to trust him to protect me.

I did trust him. Yet I'd been more or less on my own for so long, it was going to be hard to break some of the habits I'd learned out of self-preservation. Shivering, I remembered the first time he left for work without setting my clothes out for the day. Too frozen with indecision, I'd called in sick.

The first time we went out for supper and he was too busy with business emails to order my food. I ended up pointing at something on the menu, not realizing it was food I didn't like.

With full knowledge and consent, I'd let him make me helpless and unable to function for weeks. The only thing that snapped me out of it was the very real possibility of inpatient psychiatric care when my therapist finally realized how much weight I'd lost.

"Knock it off, hooker," I muttered under my breath. It wouldn't happen again. I wouldn't let it, but I'd eventually have to share what I'd gone through. It wasn't entirely his fault, and I knew better than to start assigning blame. It was a losing game.

"Knock what off?" Henry asked, coming in for the food.

"Nothing," I said, too quickly. When he gave me a suspicious look, I added, "There was a fly buzzing around. I told him to knock it off."

His glance fell on the clothes in my arms. "Ah, yeah, the bugs are already out. Thanks for bringing us something to wear."

"May I dress, Master?" How many times had I asked him that? The answer was usually no if we were going to be staying in.

"Oh, baby girl," he whispered, sliding a finger under the steel training collar that was growing surprisingly comfortable. "Thank you for asking. Yes, get dressed. I don't want bugs chewing on your gorgeous body."

"Yes, Master, thank you."

Tipping up my chin, he kissed me. "Besides, chewing on your gorgeous body is my job, and I'm a jealous man."

A quick jolt of arousal coursed down my spine and I shivered, then dressed as quick as I could. "Can I carry anything?"

"Nope. I got it, but you could grab a bottle of wine from the downstairs refrigerator and a couple of glasses. Also, get your phone. It's in the drawer under the microwave."

I blinked, remembering my promise to text Charles. "Sh…sugar. Charles asked me to text him when I got home. He must be worried sick."

"I took care of it, then turned it off so it should have a full charge, but you might want to check for missed calls. Your car keys are with it, and I took the liberty of putting your house key back on the ring."

He walked out with the food and a couple of plates, leaving me with everything I'd need to go back to my life.

I could go to my tiny studio loft in downtown Minneapolis.

And pack up your shit.

Go have a drink at the bistro down the street from my building.

On the way to pack up your shit.

See what Charles was up to.

To ask him for help packing up your shit.

My inner self had definite opinions. Smiling wryly, I powered up my phone. There were only a few messages, one of which was from Patrick with a list of things he wanted for Stronghold's dungeon. I smiled and saved it for later. For a man who said he wasn't going to purchase another series, he was already looking at five figures.

Another was Charles asking where I wanted the sale proceeds deposited. I replied with a short message telling him I'd be in touch. Because I was an idiot, I hadn't even thought about bank accounts. I'd need one if I was going to start a real business. Henry would know what to do, but I needed to learn to do it myself.

Grabbing the wine and a couple of glasses, I went back upstairs to join him.

"Hey, sweetheart. Any urgent messages?"

"No, not really. Just one from Charles wanting to know where to deposit my cut of the sales, plus another from Patrick ordering about ten thousand dollars' worth of bondage furniture."

"Holy crap! That's amazing. I'm sure you already have business financial matters straightened out." He took the wine from me, leaving me with the glasses as we walked outside to face a gorgeous pink and purple sunset. "And if I forgot to tell you, congratulations on your success. I'd love to say I knew you could do it, but I truly didn't, and I'm sorry."

"It's all right. I didn't exactly show you what I was working on, and—"

"I never went into your studio, same as you never went into the game room."

"Yeah."

He wrapped an arm around my shoulder as we walked toward the fire pit near the small koi pond. All the fish were long dead, but we kept it filtered with a small fountain and the frogs were fun to watch. Maybe someday… I shook the thought away. We had more important things to talk about.

The scent of late blooming roses turned the air sweet and fragrant. They'd grown a little wild in the last few months, the canes rangy and thin. A good pruning would put them to rights for the winter.

We walked past the rose arbor and my feet stalled. Henry had erected our old dining fly with a free-standing hammock inside. Amply sized for two, we'd spent many hours cuddled up in it just talking while the sun set, but we hadn't used it in years. Scattered with pillows and plush throws, it looked inviting and comfortable.

A white sheet hung between two trees, positioned in front of his laptop and a small projector. The food was arranged on trays, along with cut vegetables, fruit, and dipping sauces.

"Dinner and a show," he pronounced, tapping a button on his phone. The sound of ocean waves echoed from tiny speakers set around the hammock. "And the beach. What do you think?"

"Oh. My. God." I turned in a circle, looking at everything he'd done. "It's just like our trip to Myrtle Beach."

"Well, with better food anyway. We can skip the hot dogs."

"No, I want one." Turning to him, I hugged him, laying my head on his chest. "This is amazing. Thank you, Master."

"You're welcome, baby. Want to help me get the fire started?"

"Sure." Kneeling next to the fire pit, I set a fireplace lighter to the tinder he'd laid. The dry wood caught quickly and I sat back on my heels as he fed larger pieces into the burgeoning campfire. "This is really nice."

"Thanks. I'm glad you like it." Taking my hand, he helped me stand, then led me to the table full of food. There was only one chair, with a cushion laid on the grass next to it. Sitting down, he gestured at the cushion, asking me to kneel at his feet.

When I obeyed, he stroked my head, brushing a few strands of hair from my face. "We're going to eat and discuss how you see our relationship." He picked up a carrot, then swirled it through ranch dressing and held it out for me.

I ate it from his hand, the familiar ritual both poignant and bitingly bitter. "I honestly don't know. It's..." I let out a breath and accepted a thin slice of red bell pepper wrapped around a piece of feta cheese. "I'm not the same person I used to be."

"No, neither of us are," he murmured, touching my lips with a napkin. "I guess the easiest way is to start off with things we used to do, and you'll tell me if you still want them."

"What about what you want?"

Bending down, he met my eyes. "I want you to be happy. That's it. I need you to tell me what I have to do to make that happen."

CHAPTER TWELVE

Henry

Natalie tucked her chin and chewed on her lower lip. It was a familiar response to being asked a question she didn't want to answer. We might be negotiating a new dynamic, but I'd known her tells for years.

"No picking out my clothes or ordering food for me," she finally said.

"Care to tell me why?" We hadn't done that in ages. The last time I laid out an outfit for her, she left it on the bed and wore something else. Unfortunately, I'd been too busy with work to call her on it. I couldn't remember the last time we'd gone out for a meal together.

Her mouth tightened and she shook her head. "Yellow."

"Okay." I tried to push my disappointment down. I didn't care about those old rituals, but her refusal to speak bothered me. "How about feeding you?" I asked, holding out another carrot.

"Planned scenes." She took the carrot from my fingers. "You must have better things to do with your time."

"No, I actually don't. Retired, remember?" I fed her a piece of cheese on a cracker, then made another for myself.

She let out a breath, refusing the cucumber spear dipped in bleu cheese dressing. "Okay. I can do this." Looking up at me, she said, "I could ask you the same question. How do you see our relationship? What will make you happy?"

"I want to take care of you and meet your needs, both physical and emotional."

"You're okay with not picking my clothes or food?"

"I enjoyed it, but I stopped when you didn't want it."

"Didn't want it…" She leaped to her feet and swiped at me, knocking a piece of broccoli from my hand. "Do you have any fucking clue what you did to me?"

"No, honey. I just followed your—"

Her face turned red and she hissed out an ugly laugh. "No, Henry, you don't get to do this. You trained me to lean on you. I let you manage my life to the point I couldn't fucking dress myself. The last time we went out to eat, you didn't choose my meal because you were busy with stupid email, and I didn't know what to do." Her voice softened and she turned away. "I won't let you do that again."

My stomach tightened and roiled, the few bites of food I'd had threatening to make a reappearance. Had I done that to her? Why hadn't she said anything?

"Oh, sweetheart." I reached for her and she jerked away. "I'm sorry."

Tears sparked in her eyes, but she lifted her chin and pinned me with an angry, hurt glare. "I was almost hospitalized because I couldn't eat unless you were giving it to me. I can't… I'm sorry, but I can't go back there."

"Why didn't you tell me?"

Misery wafting from her, she sank to her cushion, her shoulders hunched. "I did. You told me I was allowed to be a grownup, so I taught myself how all over again."

I wanted to go back in time and punch myself in the face. Why hadn't I noticed she was having problems? Sure, I had work, and aside from the fertility treatments, Natalie had been dealing with the restructuring of her school district. We were both so busy, we barely had time to share meals. That wasn't an excuse for not meeting her needs. It was no wonder she tried to leave.

Reaching down, I helped Natalie to her feet, then hauled her into my lap, holding her tight against me. Cupping her cheek, I made her look at me. "I was an idiot," I said firmly. "Even if we needed to change our dynamic, there was no excuse for me to let you suffer like that, and the only thing I can do is ask for your forgiveness and promise you it will never happen again."

"I've already forgiven you. Besides, it's my fault too. I didn't know how to make you listen."

"I'm listening now." I kissed her temple, inhaling her sweet scent. "I want to suggest a new ritual for us."

"What kind of ritual?"

"Every Saturday, we'll have Myrtle Beach time. We'll talk about our week, our scenes, and problems if they come up. You'll get a free pass to swear at me, yell, throw things if you want. But you have to meet me halfway. You have to tell me when I'm not meeting your expectations."

She blinked, her eyes clearing of the tears about to fall. "I... Okay. Myrtle Beach time. From sunset to dawn on Saturdays."

"Good. I also want you to journal your thoughts and feelings, good, bad, or indifferent. I'll do one too."

Lips turning down, she said, "My therapist always wanted me to do that. It felt dumb."

When had she started seeing a therapist? I pushed the question away. It didn't matter as long as she was getting help. "Are they kink-friendly?" I asked. "Maybe we could go together."

"I don't see her regularly anymore. I can schedule sessions if I need them, but we decided I was competent enough to eat and dress by myself.

"You always were, honey. You just…forgot it for a little while."

She looked down and nodded. "I guess. I should have said something. I think that was the most important thing I needed to learn from her."

"What's that?"

"That no husband or dom is a mind-reader. I can't expect you to know what I need unless I tell you." Laughing softly, she added, "Even if that means I have to tie you to your own spanking bench to make you listen."

I arched a brow, thanking my lucky stars she felt comfortable enough to tease. "Really?"

"Her words, not mine. She had a point though. I didn't go that extra step and make sure you heard me."

"I'm listening now, and I promise, I won't stop."

"And I promise I'll tell you," she murmured, resting her head against my chest.

I held her quietly for a few minutes, letting her relax against me. "I want you to have a free space."

"I don't understand what you mean by that."

"A neutral zone where our dynamic doesn't go. I'm thinking your studio."

"Will you have one too?"

"Yes. I'm going to turn your old studio into my new game room." When she frowned and opened her mouth to speak, I laid a finger over her lips. "It needs to be a new room," I said sternly. "Not what was supposed to be our nursery. We'll discuss what to do with it some other time."

"Are you saying we can't go into each other's personal space?"

"Not at all. Those are just going to be rooms where I'm not your master, and you're not my slave. I want you to have time and space to be independent to make sure you never go through what I did to you again."

Natalie

I stroked his cheek, loving the feel of his soft beard. "We, Henry. Not just you, and it doesn't do any good to blame each other over something that wouldn't have happened if I'd said something and made you listen."

His jaw tightened under my fingers, but he nodded. "There's only one rule to those spaces. You're not allowed to hide in them to avoid talking to me."

Smiling, I shook my head. I would have liked to think I wouldn't have tried it, but I knew better. This was what I wanted, and what Martine always said I needed, so I couldn't complain. "And this place on Saturday nights will be our Myrtle Beach."

"Yes. We'll think of something else for winter, but we'll have hot dogs without buns and share our weekly journals." Henry went silent for a few seconds, then added, "I suppose this will be a neutral zone too. No punishments or scenes. We'll use this time to reflect and talk."

I reached over and nipped his ear. "We used to make love in this hammock. Think a couple of old farts can still make it happen without breaking a hip?"

Laughing, he swatted at my butt. "Imp. We're not that old. That actually brings up something else I wanted to talk to you about. Would you mind me going to the gym with you?"

"No, of course not." I chewed on my lip, then sat up to face him. "Why now? I mean, you've never wanted to go before."

He took my hand and laid it on his stomach. "Remember when I used to have a six-pack? I'm thinking I have to keep an eye on my figure so you will too. Besides, you about kicked my ass when I kidnapped you, so I need to get back in shape."

I choked out a laugh, covering my mouth before I spit on him. "Oh, my God, Henry, you could make bread with that much corn."

"Nope, no buns with our hot dogs." He helped me out of the hammock and handed me a campfire fork. "We've already had our discussion about our dynamic. Let's roast weenies and make s'mores."

"And a movie," I added, pointing at the projector. "What are we watching?"

"It's a surprise."

I hadn't had one in years, but that hot dog eaten straight off a campfire fork with spicy stadium mustard instead of yellow from a plastic packet was about the best thing I'd ever eaten. Laughing together, we made a mess with the pie irons, bread, and cherry pie filling, then ate our crispy failures along with toasted marshmallows.

When we finished eating, we settled into the hammock and Henry poured wine into two glasses.

Handing me one, he said, "Ready to watch a movie?"

"Sure." I leaned back against his chest and took a sip from my glass. Tears pricked my eyes at his thoughtfulness. Not only had he recreated our happiest memory, he remembered my favorite wine. Blinking furiously, I asked, "What are we watching?"

He pointed the remote at the projector, and the familiar opening credits of *Young Frankenstein* appeared on the sheet hung before us. I wanted to protest at first. This movie was the cause of some of our earliest disagreements, yet it wasn't the film specifically.

It was me and my insecurities. My unwillingness to rise above my juvenile impulses and settle into the M/s dynamic I said I wanted.

Henry brushed a few strands of hair away from my face. "Are you okay, baby girl?"

"Yeah. I was…" I set my wine aside and lowered my head to his shoulder. "I was just thinking how dumb I was to laugh every time I called you Master before."

"Not dumb," he replied, tapping my nose. "It's funny as hell. The whole movie is, but we can watch something else. Maybe *The Holy Grail*?"

"No, this is okay."

Martine would be so proud of me. I was being proactive and forcing myself to create new associations with something old and pleasantly familiar.

Henry fell asleep halfway through the film, but I let it play until it was done. He was right. It was still funny. I turned and curled up into his embrace. I laughed at Marty playing Igor, but didn't associate it with me anymore. Why had I even done that in the first place? So stupid. Careful not to rock the hammock, I got up and turned everything off, putting the electronics safely back in the house in case it rained overnight. The rest would wait until tomorrow.

I slid in next to him, inhaling his warm masculine scent. My eyes fell closed and I yawned. Nestled in the embrace of the man I loved, I fell asleep.

***

The sound of birds woke me and I cracked an eye open, astonished to find I'd slept the night through. The kitchen door slammed and I turned over. Carrying two coffee cups, Henry walked down the deck stairs and strode toward me, a beaming smile on his face.

"Good morning, sleeping beauty." He handed me a cup, along with my cell phone. "You got a call while I was making coffee. I let it go to voicemail."

"Okay." I took a sip, then swiped the screen to wake it. Blinking in shock at the time, I looked up at him. "Why did you let me sleep so late?"

"I've only been up for about ten minutes myself. I figured you needed the rest."

"Yeah, I guess," I replied, bringing up the call log. "That was Charles. Do you mind if I call him back?"

"Nope. In fact, if you're up for it, we can drive into town, pack up your…" He shrugged and gave me a wry smile. "Apartment? House? Don't tell me it's a bench at the bus station or I'll have to spank you."

Laughing, I shook my head. "No, I got a loft apartment in the warehouse district downtown. It's a nice building with a doorman and monitored parking."

He took a sip of coffee and stared at me over the rim of his cup. "Fancy place. Then again, you can afford it if your work sells like it did last night."

"No, I really can't." I finished my drink and set the cup aside. "I got a three-month lease, but it's freakishly expensive for a loft the size of our kitchen. I just…"

"What is it, honey?" He took my hand and kissed my knuckles.

"Remember Dayton's on Eighth and Nicollet?" When he nodded, I said, "My parents used to take me and my sisters to visit Santa and look at the window displays. I always thought it was the most beautiful building, and I kind of made a promise to myself that I'd live in one like it someday."

"And you did it." He pulled me into a tight hug and kissed the top of my head. "I'm proud of you, baby girl."

"Nope." I extricated myself from the hammock, biting back a groan at the crick in my back. "I slept there for a total of two nights before you absconded with me like a Victorian highwayman."

"Is your name on the lease?"

"Well, yes, but—"

"Then you live there." He cocked his head and scanned the back yard, then started cleaning up our mess. "Let's get this taken care of, then I have to pack."

"Where are you going?" Seriously? Was he planning on taking off for another trip now of all times?

"We're going to stay in your loft for three months while we fix up your new studio, lay carpet, and…" He pulled me close with an arm around my waist. "I have an idea for the spare bedroom, but we're going to talk about it first."

"What's your idea?"

"Remember that posh bathroom and walk-in closet you always wanted?"

My feet stalled as we reached the steps. "Are you serious?"

He grinned crookedly, his cheeks turning red. "It depends. Do you think it's a good idea?"

"It's going to cost a fortune."

"Taken care of. I'm exercising my stock options."

"But—"

He cupped my chin and kissed me. "Natalie, don't think about the money. If you don't like the idea, say so and we'll drop it."

I bit my lip and looked up into his earnest face, unsure how I felt. I wasn't going to have a baby, and looking at that room would just be a lingering reminder of disappointment—especially if it was empty.

"I love it. Let's build ourselves a bathroom."

CHAPTER THIRTEEN

Henry

Oh, thank fuck. Picking Natalie up off her feet, I swung her around, making her giggle. When was the last time I heard her laugh with such undiluted joy?

I had to make sure though. As we were packing up the last of the mess from our impromptu campout, I said, "Remember, this is your decision. If you change your mind, we don't have to do it. It's just something I thought we'd both enjoy."

"It's perfect, really, but we're not going to get carried away and spend a truckload of money on it, okay?"

Nodding, I disassembled the dining fly while she worked on the hammock. "We'll make it happen," I promised. "We'll spend the next few days in home improvement stores, and I'll call around for some bids, but you have something to do first."

"What's that?"

"Call Charles back."

Flushing, she lowered her head. "I can't," she muttered. "I don't have a business account set up. I guess I... Never mind."

"Out with it, Natalie. No holding back anymore."

She rolled her eyes at the authority in my voice, but I wasn't about to let her fall back into old habits of keeping things from me.

"I didn't expect anything to sell."

Part of me wanted to spank her for her lack of

self-confidence, but I was too damned proud of what she'd accomplished. "Even if you hadn't sold a single thing, you tried. And your next show will be even bigger."

"Thanks." Her lips curled into a tentative smile. "I'm so glad you'll be with me for the next one."

Coughing, I cleared my throat of the emotion choking me. "Let's get this stuff put away, and we'll go out for breakfast."

"I think... Master, can we stay here, please?"

"Why? I thought you'd want to get out of the house for a few hours."

"Yes, I mean no." She shuffled her feet on the concrete garage floor and helped me put the hammock back on its shelf. "I just thought, we have all that food, and... I want to be in the basement today."

"Okay." I pulled the chain leash from my pocket and got my head into dom space. The shift in my mindset came easier every time she called me Master. "Strip for me, baby girl."

"Yes, Master." Her shoulders relaxed as she walked into the kitchen and undressed, folding her T-shirt and sweats into a neat pile on the table.

Although the sound of her calling me Master sent a punch of desire through my chest and down into my balls, I wasn't sure this was the right time for us to be playing. Maybe it was what we needed though. We had a new set of ground rules and better understanding of each other. The more I thought about the idea, the better I liked it. Natalie and I could explore protocol today to figure out what worked and what didn't.

It was almost exactly what I intended when I kidnapped her, but with more negotiation. Quickly shaking the thought away, I snapped the chain on her collar. I wasn't proud of myself for what I'd done, and counted myself lucky she forgave me.

Lowering her eyes, she put her arms behind her back and grasped her elbows, then spread her feet apart. The ring in her clit hood flashed at me, and it was all I could do to stop myself from laying her across the kitchen table to devour her sweet pussy.

"Let's go downstairs, baby."

"Yes, Master," she murmured, her right arm falling to the bannister. "Is it okay if I kneel on the pillow?"

I followed her down the stairs, my eyes fixed on her round backside. "Please do. I don't want your knees on concrete. We'll figure something out until we get carpet installed."

"Thank you." She glided across the floor, then gracefully knelt on the cushion facing me.

Her position was textbook perfect. Eyes still cast down, her arms were up, fingers laced together behind her head. Sitting back on her heels, she spread her thighs apart, revealing droplets of moisture on her pussy.

"God, you're beautiful," I whispered.

A heavy knock sounded on the front door upstairs and I frowned irritably at the noise.

"Are you expecting a delivery, Master?"

"No." The knock sounded again and I bent to kiss her cheek. "Stay here and I'll get rid of them."

Grumbling under my breath, I stomped up the stairs and opened the door to reveal a pair of police officers, one man and one woman, who both had their hands resting on sidearms.

"Can I help you, officers?"

"Are you Henry Mercer?" the male officer asked.

"Yes, sir. What's this about?"

"We have a warrant to search your house for evidence of a crime." He held up a document, but pulled it away before I could read more than the first paragraph.

I let out a breath and straightened my shoulders, then stepped away from the door. It was time to pay the piper for kidnapping Natalie. "Of course. Please, come in, but give me a few minutes to make sure my wife is dressed."

Instead of listening, they pushed past me and headed straight for the basement. I followed them, rage boiling at the thought of them seeing her. I should have been more worried about the possibility of jail time, but it wasn't as important as protecting my wife.

Natalie kept her position, hands behind her head, thighs splayed wide, but her lips tightened with fury. "Henry, I swear to God, if this is your idea—"

"No." I grabbed a sheet from the bed, then helped her to her feet and wrapped it around her. "I have no idea what's going on. They have a warrant to search the house."

"Sick fuck," the female officer muttered, looking at my impact play implements hung on the wall. Judging by the way she lowered her eyes and looked away, I was sure she hadn't intended for me to hear her.

Turning Natalie toward the stairs, I said, "Go upstairs, baby."

"Do you think someone saw…" Pressing her lips together, she shook her head. "We're both going upstairs. Now."

There was a time and place for a M/s dynamic. A submissive gave over power at their will. Natalie had taken hers back, and I had no problem letting her.

When we reached the top of the stairs, she grabbed the clothes she'd left on the kitchen table and dressed, then picked up her phone.

"Let's go outside. We need to talk, and I have to make a call."

"Who are you calling?" I shut the door behind us, then followed her down the driveway until we were several yards from the house.

She tapped the screen, then pressed her phone to her ear. "Charles. I think he might have seen..." She straightened and tapped again, putting the call on speaker. "Hey, Charles, I'm returning your call. You're on speaker and my husband is with me."

"Oh, my! Does that mean you two crazy kids are back together?"

Smiling warmly at me, Natalie said, "Yeah. We've had a couple of days to work things out and—"

"Splendid news, darling. It's a pleasure to meet you, Henry. We'll have to get together for lunch soon."

"Thanks, but that's not why I—"

"I'm afraid I have to run. I'm having brunch with a lovely chap I met at the pub the other day. We'll chat later, but I'm so happy for you both. Ta!"

The call dropped and Natalie slipped the phone into her pocket. "Okay, so we know Charles isn't the one who tattled about you kidnapping me. That means someone else did, but since I'm obviously here of my own free will, they can't do anything. We'll just tell them it was a game between consenting adults."

I frowned, then shook my head. "I don't know. If they were here because someone saw me take you, they'd have been more concerned about getting you away from me."

"What else could it be?"

Natalie

Seated in the porch swing on the deck, I leaned against Henry's shoulder while we waited for the police to finish ransacking my house. It was violating on a deeply personal level to have strangers go through our private space.

"May I ask a question, Master?"

"Of course, baby. Ask anything you want."

"Why did they start in the basement and not somewhere else?"

He frowned and absentmindedly kissed the top of my head. "No idea. Maybe they work from bottom to top."

"What's taking them so long? It's been almost two hours." Patience wasn't one of my gifts. I hated waiting.

He hugged me tighter against his chest, then set the swing moving again. "It's a big house, baby girl. I'm sure they'll tell us what's going on soon."

The French door from the kitchen opened suddenly, revealing the two officers who interrupted our morning with their nonsense. The taller of the two, a man with a shaved head and skin the color of mahogany, approached us. According to his name badge, he was Officer Daniels.

"Mr. Mercer, we'd like you to come to the station with us to answer a few questions."

"With all due respect, sir, what's this about?" I asked, ignoring the warning squeeze Henry gave my hand.

"Our interest is in Mr. Mercer, ma'am. If he cooperates, we won't have to involve you at all."

I blinked in surprise at the implied threat. "You

don't have a warrant for either one of us."

Officer Reynolds, a woman with freckles and red hair slicked back into a tight bun, said, "We can get them easily enough. As long as Mr. Mercer comes with us now, we can avoid all that unpleasantness."

What the hell? Henry was right. If this was about him kidnapping me, they definitely would have wanted me to come to the station with them. It didn't make sense, but I couldn't think of what else might bring the police to our door on a Sunday morning.

Henry stood, pressing on my shoulder to keep me in my seat. "All right. Give me a few minutes to change and I'll follow you. My wife will stay here."

"Sir, you can ride in the cruiser."

"Is he under arrest?" I asked, brushing his hand aside so I could stand. There was no way I was going to step aside and let him put himself at risk over me.

"No, ma'am, but—"

"Then we'll drive ourselves."

"Natalie, I can—"

Spinning around, I stabbed a finger in his chest and glared up at him. "No. We're going to lawyer up and get to the bottom of this fuckery together."

I hid a wince, knowing my ass was going to pay for both the f-bomb and for ordering Henry around like I was his domme. The one thing he'd asked of me was to quit swearing and I'd already blown it. I absolutely hated having punishments hanging over me, and it might be hours before we'd have time to attend to it.

Instead of arching a brow into his patented angry dom stare, he smiled and kissed my forehead. "Yes, ma'am."

God, I loved him so much. How could I have ever left him?

Both officers wore ugly scowls, but let us go inside to make ourselves presentable. I wasn't the slightest bit upset at their disappointment. Without warrants for our arrests, they couldn't do shit.

There wasn't much help for me, but Henry put on a green button-down shirt and a pair of khaki trousers he wore on the rare times we went somewhere nice. I did my best with some lip gloss and mascara from my purse. I wasn't willing to leave Henry to drive to the loft for something else.

"I feel like I'm wearing pajamas to a dinner party," I muttered, yanking the waistband of my sweats up over my hips.

As he was threading his belt through the loops on his trousers, he asked, "Hey, did you pack the stuff from the closet in your old studio? I think you had clothes in there."

"No, I completely forgot. I'll see what I have." I strode down the hall and into the other room, then threw open the closet door. Thankfully, there was an old sundress and shoes to match, along with a slightly pilled cardigan. I dressed as quickly as I could, and within minutes, we were on the road following the police car.

Fumbling with my phone, I brought up the number for Gina Rivera, the attorney handling my divorce. I needed to tell her Henry and I were back together anyway, and she'd know someone who could represent us.

"Who are you calling?" Henry asked, his eyes fixed on the road.

"My lawyer." The call connected, and after her soft greeting, I said, "Hi Gina, I have two things for you. The first is that Henry and I are back together, so you can cancel the divorce proceedings."

"Congratulations, Natalie. I'm so pleased to hear that. What's the second thing?"

"Two police officers came to the house with a warrant to search our property this morning. We think someone saw us... Well, part of me making up with Henry involved him kidnapping me after my gallery show."

Coughing, Gina cleared her throat. "And you're back with him...why?"

"Yeah, it was a shitty idea, and Henry would be the first to admit it. I forgave him though, and I honestly think it was the best thing he could have done to make me see his side of the story."

Henry's face reddened and I chuckled. Whoops. There was another swear, but maybe Henry would take pity on me because of this completely fucked-up day. There should be dispensation when the police bust down the playroom door.

"I see." Gina went silent for a few seconds. "Are you currently in danger, Natalie?"

"No, not at all. We talked and it was..." I looked at my husband and laid a hand on his arm. "It was really good. I'm happy."

"Well, okay then. I make it a point to never delve into the inner workings of a marriage. That's for your therapist. Did the police tell you what they were searching for?"

"No. We thought it was because someone saw him kidnap me, but the officers didn't have any interest in me. They tried to threaten Henry with a warrant for me if he didn't comply, so I...we decided we needed representation. Can you recommend someone who can meet us at the station? We're on our way now."

"I can meet you there. This isn't my specialty, but the presence of an attorney will usually make the police back down. My wife Samantha handles criminal defense, so I'll bring her along. Do not say a word until I get there. All you have to do is politely refuse to answer any questions."

"Got it. Thanks, Gina."

CHAPTER FOURTEEN

Henry

"What did she say?" I asked as Natalie tucked her phone in her purse.

I hated having her involved in whatever this was. It went against everything I believed to expose her to anything harmful, but there was going to be another fight if I tried to make her stay home. Now that she had her mojo back, I wasn't about to stifle her.

"She'll meet us, and told us to refuse to answer any questions until she got there."

"All right."

"Yeah. I'm thinking the police are looking for something they don't think a lawyer will let them have. That would explain their attempt to question you without an attorney."

Her thoughts mirrored mine, but I had no idea what they'd be after. Aside from kidnapping my wife, I hadn't gotten so much as a parking ticket in years. Nerves twitched in my belly as I turned into the parking lot. Even knowing I'd done nothing wrong, it was impossible to feel calm equanimity when faced with police questioning.

I backed into a spot, then stopped the engine and listened to it tick as it cooled. "Are you ready?" I finally asked.

"Nope," she replied, popping her lips on the end of the word as she played Sudoku on her phone. "We're going to sit tight until Gina gets here. She drives a red Miata."

"Christ, Natalie!" I pushed my hands through my hair, unable to control my agitation. "How the hell are you being so damned calm?"

"I'm not." She tapped the screen and a chime sounded, announcing her success. "I'm terrified, and if I move, I'll probably puke down the side of your car."

"Oh, baby girl, c'mere." Unfastening my seatbelt, I reached over and pulled her into my arms. "We're going to be okay, I swear it."

I had to pull myself together for her. I made a promise to her and to myself to protect her and I couldn't do it if I was losing my shit.

She sniffed and buried her face in my chest. "I'm sorry. Just… I need a minute."

A sharp tap sounded on the hood of my car and I looked up, then scowled and rolled down the window.

"Can we help you?" I asked, trying to remain polite.

"This isn't the place for one of your sex games, Mr. Mercer. Will you come inside so we can get started?" Officer Daniels glared at me, and I resisted the urge to punch him.

I gritted my teeth and let out a breath through my nose. "I—"

"We'll come in with our lawyer," Natalie replied, not bothering to keep the derision from her tone. "If you don't have a warrant, you can wander off and—"

"I'm Gina Rivera, and I'll be representing the Mercers along with my partner, Samantha Rivera."

The officer swore under his breath and walked away, and I nodded my thanks to the young woman.

Smiling, she juggled an infant in her arms and crouched to peer in the car window. "Hey, Natalie.

Sorry, but I had to bring the rugrat. The nanny has Sundays off."

"Hi, little man!"

I wanted to stop her, but Natalie got out of the car and rounded the trunk, opening her arms to accept the baby. It broke my heart every time she held someone else's child, knowing she'd never get one of her own.

"How is he doing? Feels like he's gained some weight since you brought him home." She opened the blanket, revealing a baby with a wild shock of blond hair.

"Two pounds," Samantha said, beaming. "Caleb loves sweet potatoes."

Natalie handed the little boy back to his mothers. "Okay, now that I've gotten my baby cuddles out of the way, we should go in before the officers standing by the door explode."

"All right," Gina replied, suddenly businesslike despite the burp cloth over one shoulder. "I'll be with you, Natalie, and Samantha will go in with Henry. She has more experience with criminal proceedings, and we both feel he's the target."

"And remember, not a word unless we give you permission to answer," Samantha added. "Give no more information than you absolutely have to, but answer honestly."

"No," I said, wrapping an arm around Natalie's waist. "We're not going to be separated."

"You won't have a choice," Gina said. "They're going to question you separately. All you have to do is let Samantha and I do our jobs. We'll find out what this is all about, and get you back home before you know it."

"Assuming you're innocent of whatever they're trying to prove you did," Samantha replied.

"Considering I have no idea what they're going to accuse me of, I'd say that's a safe bet," I snapped.

"Are we ready?" Gina asked.

No. "Let's get this done."

"Let the fuckery commence!" Natalie shouted, staring directly at the officers hovering like crows in front of the door.

"Baby girl—"

"I know," she said, breezing by me. "You're going to spank me later, but... Yeah, sorry, not sorry."

I choked out a laugh and rubbed my face. This was the Natalie I remembered. "God, I love you."

Grinning at me, she tossed her hair over her shoulder. "Love you back, baby boy. Let's get this done so we can go back to what we were doing."

Natalie

I'd somehow managed to put a good face on things so I didn't make Henry worry, but I felt like I was going to throw up. The smell of industrial disinfectant assailed my nostrils as the officers walked us inside. I got the distinct impression we'd have been cuffed and frog-marched into jail cells if Samantha and Gina hadn't been with us.

Our lawyers had been right. We were separated almost immediately and forced to empty our pockets, then led to different interview rooms. I sat in the uncomfortable plastic chair, then held my arms out for Caleb when Gina tried to juggle both her son and her briefcase with limited success.

"Ugh!" Gina passed him to me, brushing disheveled hair out of her eyes. "Thanks for holding him. He throws a fit if we put him in his carrier."

"No problem." I let out a breath, disgusted with myself for needing a fucking teddy bear in the form of my lawyer's baby.

Officer Daniels walked in, followed by a woman in a suit. A badge hung at her waist, but I couldn't read it.

"Mrs. Mercer, I'm Detective Rachel Whalen," the woman said, sitting across from me. "We have just a few questions, but I'm sure we can get you on your way soon."

I nodded, reminding myself to keep my damned mouth shut. I didn't have much of a verbal filter on a good day.

"Where were you this past Friday night?"

"You'll have to be more specific, Detective," Gina replied, straightening in her chair.

"Very well. Mrs. Mercer, where were you between the hours of eleven o'clock Friday night and four on Saturday morning?"

"Give only enough information to answer the question, Natalie," Gina said.

"I was at home with my husband." I settled Caleb in my arms and crooned a soft melody to soothe him.

"Do you have anyone who can confirm that?"

"No."

"All right." Detective Whalen opened a folder, then pushed a piece of paper toward me. "This is divorce paperwork filed by you six days ago. If you were planning to leave your husband, why were you with him?"

"The question is irrelevant. Don't answer."

The detective scowled, but smoothed her face quickly. "All right. That's all I have for now. You can wait here."

"Can you watch Caleb for a few minutes?" Gina asked. "I'm going to get some answers and find out what they're up to."

"Sure. No problem."

The door closed behind them and I smiled down at Caleb. "Hey, little man," I murmured.

He opened his mouth in a toothless grin and babbled at me, his tiny hands waving. I reached into Gina's diaper bag and pulled out a teething ring, then let him chew on it.

Maybe… An adopted baby would be no less mine than one I birthed from my body, right? Why hadn't Henry and I discussed the possibility? There were so many kids who needed stable homes.

I wished I had my phone. I had a voice recording app, and it seemed easier to journal my thoughts if I could hear them out loud. Then again, I had a captive audience, even if he was only six months old.

Of course, I was probably being recorded, but talking to an infant about my wish for a child of my own was harmless.

"So, what do you think? Should I talk to Henry about adopting or just let it slide? I mean, I'll be over sixty at high school graduation. Is that too weird?"

Caleb babbled at me some more and I tickled his chin. "Yeah, I think I'm going to bring it up during our next Myrtle Beach talk. Who knows? Maybe we'll bring home a little boy or girl just as cute as you are."

He grabbed at my hair, making me wince. "What? No friends for you?"

The door opened, revealing a scowling Gina. She slammed it behind her and sat next to me.

"Is something wrong?" I asked, shifting Caleb to my other shoulder.

"Yeah. You sure you were with Henry all night on Friday?"

"Yes. Why?"

"The police are investigating an assault. The victim claims it was Henry, so I need to know if he left you at any time on Friday night."

I thrust Caleb at her and barely made it to the wastebasket in time for my morning coffee to make a reappearance. He'd left me all night. I was in a cage and he was presumably upstairs.

No, it wasn't possible. He wouldn't harm another woman, but I couldn't prove it.

"Are you okay?" Gina asked, handing me a cloth from her diaper bag.

"Yeah." I wiped my face, then spat into the wastebasket. "No. He left me alone for several hours that night. I can't prove his whereabouts."

"Doesn't matter." Gina pointed at the steel slave collar still around my neck. "They'll say you were coerced anyway."

"That's bullshit."

"It is what it is. All I can say is you'd better pray Henry has a better explanation than you do."

"Maybe I do. There's a video on Henry's computer. He recorded our..." I stopped and glanced at the camera over our head. "Our reconciliation is on video, but it's... Well, let's just say it's not safe for work."

"Does it show him on camera during the whole time Detective Whalen asked about?"

"Only part of it."

"We need something better." Gina took Caleb from me and picked up her diaper bag. "You don't have anything else?"

"No. Is this going to be a problem?"

"Sit tight until I get back, and don't say a word to anyone except me or Samantha."

She walked out, leaving me alone. I didn't know

what to think. Was it possible Henry had assaulted some woman while I was locked in my cage?

I had to admit it was, but I just didn't see it happening. What man would go to the lengths Henry had to get our relationship back, only to turn around and hurt someone else?

That part was what didn't make sense. Henry might be a sadist, but he wasn't abusive, and he didn't cheat. I also didn't believe he'd have left me alone. He might not have been in the basement, but I was willing to bet he'd been monitoring me. He'd had doms blackballed from the Minneapolis scene for such carelessness.

"Once you eliminate the impossible, whatever remains, no matter how improbable, must be the truth," I murmured, quoting one of my favorite authors.

Was it possible for Henry to cheat? Yes, but unlikely.

Was it possible for him to have left the house while I was caged? Also yes, but maybe not. I tapped my chin and tried to remember. I didn't sleep much that night, and I would have heard the door if he'd left. All right, so that wasn't a possibility.

So, what did that leave me?

Stuck with too many questions and not enough answers.

Fuck.

CHAPTER FIFTEEN

Henry

"Would you say you're a gifted man, Mr. Mercer?"

Samantha frowned, but nodded her approval.

"I don't understand the question."

"Your wife is very beautiful, isn't she?"

"What's your point, Rachel?" Samantha asked. "My client is a busy man, and your questions aren't going anywhere."

"She was going to divorce you. How did that make you feel?"

"Mr. Mercer and his wife have made amends. She's asked us not to pursue a divorce. Get to the point."

Detective Whalen leaned forward and rested her elbows on the table. "See, I'm thinking you got upset. Your gorgeous wife decided to head off for greener pastures. You also recently left your job of over twenty years."

I kept silent, but couldn't help thinking that was exactly what almost happened with Natalie. They were using her to scare me. Too bad it was working.

"Irrelevant." Samantha scowled, then stood. "Are you done yet?"

"Not quite." She slid a sheet of paper across the table, then smirked at me.

Samantha pulled it close and her face darkened as she read. "Henry, do you know someone named

Bethany Thompson?"

"Yes."

"What was the nature of your relationship?"

I blinked at Samantha, then shrugged. "She was my boss for five years. Our dislike of each other was well-known."

"When did you last see her?"

"Tuesday of last week."

"Is she the reason you quit?"

"Yes. Tuesday morning, she attempted to have me demoted from a project I spent two years developing, despite finishing it under budget and six months early. I decided to retire instead, and left before lunch."

"And that's the last time you saw her?"

"No. She chased me from the building to call me some choice names. I didn't engage."

"You didn't stop to argue with her?" Detective Whalen asked. "I'd think you'd be furious."

"Actually, I'm happy about it. I'll have more time to spend with my wife. As far as Bethany is concerned, I'll be eternally grateful if I never see her again. Also, I was parked well within range of the security cameras."

The two women looked at each other, then down at several sheets of paper in a folder. "Would someone care to tell me what's going on?"

"Henry—"

"No, Samantha. I need answers. Why am I here?"

"You've been accused of sexually assaulting Bethany Thompson at approximately midnight on Friday. She says you took her into your basement and forced her to perform oral sex on you. Her description of your playroom matches what the officers found."

Was Bethany truly that vindictive? I wanted to think she wouldn't be, but I knew better. I'd left her in a bind. Sara Lyons would probably be able to take over my project, but it wouldn't happen overnight.

"No. Just flat no. The idea of touching her makes me nauseous, and I wouldn't have that woman in my house at all, much less in a private place I share with my wife."

"Then maybe you can explain how she could describe your basement so accurately," Detective Whalen said. "She's obviously been there."

"It wasn't on my invitation, I assure you," I replied, still thinking. "But maybe it was."

"Henry, do not say a word," Samantha warned.

"No." I stood and raked my hands through my hair. "I had a barbecue a few years ago and invited everyone from the department. That included Bethany because Natalie and I couldn't think of a way to exclude her. She has been in my house. I'm assuming one of my former coworkers still has pictures of the party. They might also still be up on the company website."

"All right," Detective Whalen said. "That leads us to another issue. I'm afraid you'll have to submit to a medical exam. Your accuser made certain comments about your…anatomy."

"What about his anatomy?" Samantha demanded.

Detective Whalen passed over another sheet of paper. "In her statement, Ms. Thomson says he has a stinky, uncircumcised micropenis."

"All right. We can schedule an exam for later in the week. Is my client free to go?"

"I have more questions regarding his relationship with his wife."

"No. That information has no bearing on this investigation," Samantha said.

"See, I'm having a hard time believing such

a beautiful woman would stay with a man with a smelly micropenis, and given she's filed for divorce, I'm thinking he coerced her into staying. Maybe he threatened Ms. Thompson if she didn't."

"You have no evidence, and as I've said, Mrs. Mercer no longer wishes to pursue a divorce."

"I bet we'll find Mrs. Mercer's DNA all over the basement."

"She lives there, Detective," Samantha retorted. "You're interested in whether Ms. Thompson's DNA is present, not that of the woman who owns the house."

"She moved out. Her name is on a lease for a loft downtown."

Oh, for fuck's sake. This was bullshit. If all I needed to do was drop trou... I stood and unzipped my pants.

"Mr. Mercer, what are you... Oh, my." Detective Whalen's eyes widened as she focused on my groin.

"You'll have to check medical records for details on my circumcision, I'm afraid. It probably happened before you were born. On a personal note, the presence or absence of a foreskin has no bearing on hygiene."

"I believe you've made your point," Samantha said, amusement curling her lips into a smile. "Detective, did Ms. Thompson mention anything about a Prince Albert piercing?"

"No." Detective Whalen cleared her throat and lifted her gaze to my face while I tucked myself away and zipped up. "If you'll excuse me, I need to confer with my colleagues. Please remain in this room, Mr. Mercer."

"I'm thinking if you shoved your dick in Bethany's mouth like she said, she'd have some chipped teeth,"

Samantha muttered under her breath after the door closed behind Detective Whalen.

I wasn't about to discuss the mechanics of oral sex with her, regardless of her professional curiosity. "I am very sorry about Bethany. No matter how much we disliked each other, no woman deserves to be victimized. However, since I'm obviously not the culprit, I'd like to take my wife home."

Leaning close, Samantha said, "May I ask you a personal question?"

"No. I'm not going to tell you how oral sex works with a genital piercing."

She chuckled softly and shook her head. "I wanted to know why Bethany would chase you across the parking lot."

"Because she's spiteful and mean."

"Aside from that. Did your retirement harm her in some way?"

I studied her and nodded reluctantly. I didn't want to say anything that might muddy up the investigation of the person who had assaulted Bethany. Then again, she'd been awfully specific about the circumstances.

"Probably. The person she chose to take my place has no experience with the project. She was depending on me to train my replacement. I have no idea if the person can do the work or not, nor do I care."

I chose not to mention Sara's name. Most likely, she had nothing to do with this mess, and there was no point dragging her into it. Thankfully, Samantha didn't ask.

"Hmm." Samantha got up and strode to the door. "Don't go anywhere. I'll be right back."

Natalie

Sitting still made me anxious, but pacing made me nauseous. Worse, my stupid brain was wondering if it was true.

Had my husband assaulted a woman?

No. Just hell to the no. Henry wouldn't have done that.

But he could have.

He hated Bethany. Granted, I was no great fan of hers either. The few times I'd met her, she'd been rude, arrogant, and thoroughly unpleasant to anyone she thought was beneath her—which was pretty much everyone.

I could see him not going out of his way to help her, but assault? Did he hate her enough to hurt her like that? The man I married wouldn't have touched her.

Of course, the man I married wouldn't have kidnapped me in the trunk of my own car.

The door opened, revealing Gina with Caleb sprawled across her chest fast asleep. She smiled and held out my purse and phone. "Some new evidence has come to light, which the investigators believe exonerates Henry. They have a few more questions for him, but it shouldn't take longer than an hour or so. He suggested I take you home so you don't have to wait here."

"I… Yes, please."

I followed her out, my mind still whirling as she tucked Caleb into his car seat. We got in and she started the engine, making me realize I was seated in a gray minivan instead of her cute red Miata. Yeah, baby seat. God, I was a dumbass.

"Are you okay, Natalie?" she asked.

"Yeah," I said, too quickly. "I'm fine. If I forgot to say it, thank you for coming out on your day off. Why don't we stop and I'll buy you lunch?"

"No, I'm good, but thanks. The cranky beast in the back seat is asleep, so I'm going to let him stay that way and try to get some work done."

Thankfully, she seemed willing to make small talk and didn't require me to answer hard questions during the short ride home. When we arrived, I thought about being polite and asking her inside, but she was clearly ready to get on with her day.

I waved as she drove away, then walked to the front door and let my hand rest on the knob. All the plans we made. The studio and new bathroom. Myrtle Beach nights...

Spinning around, I jogged to my car. I couldn't do this. I wasn't going to be able to look Henry in the eye and tell him I doubted him.

"Stupid, stupid, stupid," I muttered, taking a turn too fast. It wasn't even Henry. Logically, I knew he couldn't have done what they said, even before the new evidence came to light. I didn't even know what it was, but it wasn't important.

It came down to me not trusting him. I'd been married to him for almost two decades. I shouldn't need some cop telling me he was innocent.

Forty-five minutes later, I was parked in my numbered spot in the garage next to my apartment building. I wasn't even sure how I'd gotten there.

Tracing the edges of my phone, I stared off into the darkened garage without getting out while I tried to decide what to do. I swiped the phone awake and found a text from Martine asking after me.

"God help me, if I have to run crying to my

therapist over every idiotic thought in my head…" I tapped to call her.

"Hello, Natalie. I haven't heard from you in awhile, but congratulations on your gallery show. I intended to buy something, but everything was already sold by the time I got there."

"You…came to my show?"

"Of course. Your art is beautiful. I wanted Persephone for my office."

"You didn't say hello." Why was I fucking crying? I drew in a breath in an attempt to calm down, then added, "I'm so glad you came. Thank you."

"You were mobbed by people wanting your attention. I was thrilled to see how happy you were."

"Yeah, it was nuts. Anyway, you're probably wondering why I'm bugging you on a Sunday."

"No, not really. I can be in my office in about fifteen minutes. Are you close by?"

Tears fell in earnest and I coughed, trying to dislodge the knot in my throat. "I'm close."

Her voice sharpening with worry, Martine said, "Natalie, if you're driving, you need to take a little time to calm down. Remember what we worked on to control your anxiety?"

I breathed deep, wrapping my arms around myself as I tried to let go of the tension. "Yes, I remember."

"Good. Actually, I have a better idea. Is there a coffee shop or pub near you? I'll meet you there."

"I'm in the warehouse district."

"Okay. Are you close enough to walk to Spyhouse Coffee on Washington?"

Forcing my muscles to relax, I exhaled. "Yeah, I can be there in about ten minutes."

"Everything's going to be fine. We'll talk this out and help you make sense out of whatever is bothering you."

Chewing on my lip, I paced in circles outside the coffee shop. I didn't even know what I was going to tell her, but one thing I could count on with Martine was her ability to listen and sort through my whackadoodle thoughts.

She strode up to me wearing leggings and a T-shirt. Her blonde hair was tied in a pony tail reaching her shoulders. I'd never seen her dressed so casually, but I was bugging her on her day off.

"Hey, I'm glad you called," she said. "Let's get a table and some coffee."

After ordering our drinks, we found a table in a secluded corner. I rubbed my forehead and looked down at my cup. "I have no idea where to start with this."

"All right." Martine took a sip of her coffee. "You were supposed to be moving last Tuesday, right? Is that where things are going to start for you?"

"Yeah, last Tuesday." The whole story poured out of me, including the kidnapping, my reconciliation with Henry, and the drama with the police. She was quiet the whole time I talked, but passed me tissues when I needed them.

"Wow, you've had an eventful week," she finally said. "I won't ask how you were feeling when you thought you were being kidnapped, but I'm curious to know your state of mind after you found out it was Henry and resolved your differences."

"Hopeful." I drank my coffee and watched an elderly couple walk past with a small dog. "Happy, excited, like anything was possible."

"Good, those are all positive, and I adore Henry's Myrtle Beach idea. Is that how you saw your relationship in the past before you started having problems?"

I smiled wistfully. "Yeah, it was just like we used to be."

"Including your level of intimacy?"

"No, that was better."

Martine chuckled softly. "That's good to know." Peering at me over the rim of her cup, she continued, "Henry is a sadist, and there's nothing wrong with that between consenting partners as long as he abides by your safewords."

"And I'm a masochist. Match made in heaven, right?"

"It can be, if you're able to safeword before he goes too far, and he listens." She leaned back in her chair. "Given his unorthodox method of getting you back, would you say he was capable of what the police wanted to accuse him of?"

"No. Absolutely not." My coffee was cold, but I drank it anyway, needing time to allow one damned coherent thought to rise to the surface. "Henry is all about the safeword. His most annoying habit is stopping a scene for yellow. It's just...I feel violated. The police searched our playroom for almost two hours. Then I find out that horrible woman had been in our private space. I feel so fucking stupid because none of that is Henry's fault."

"Natalie, whether you think they have value or not, your feelings aren't wrong or right. They're just feelings, and you can't control them."

"But I can control how I react to them," I murmured, parroting words she'd said so many times before.

"Have you talked to Henry about what you're feeling?"

"Not yet. I... I didn't know what to say.

Everything I came up with was hurtful."

"To you, or to him?"

"Yes! What am I supposed to tell him?" I choked out a laugh, then said, "Hey, Master, I did a runner because for a minute there I thought you really had committed this crime, then I felt stupid and guilty because I know you wouldn't."

"Have you considered telling him exactly that?"

I bit my lip, then shook my head. "Do you think I should?"

She finished her coffee, then passed me another tissue. "You have to make that decision for yourself, Natalie. I can't put words into your mouth, but I can tell you that honestly sharing what you were thinking will be most helpful."

"It sounds so dumb, though." I sighed and rubbed my face, then stood. "But dumb or not, I'm going to try it. Thanks for meeting with me on such short notice. In the future, I'll try to contain my meltdowns to office hours."

Laughing, she walked out with me. "It's no trouble. I was actually thinking about stopping by for a latte anyway. But call my office next week, and we'll set up an appointment for you and Henry if he's willing to see me."

"We already talked about it, and he'd like that."

"Good. I look forward to meeting him."

I trudged back to my car, knowing she was right. It was time for big girl panties.

CHAPTER SIXTEEN

Henry

"All right, Mr. Mercer, you're free to go. Thank you for answering our questions, and for your patience in this matter." Detective Whalen handed me my wallet, phone, and keys, then opened the door to release me.

"What will happen to Bethany?" I didn't actually care, but I was curious. Accusing an innocent person of sexual assault had to carry some consequences.

"That's confidential, but we'll be in touch if we need additional information from you."

Samantha walked me out, then handed me a business card when we reached my car. "Call me if they want you to come in again," she said. "Natalie also has my wife's number."

"I will." I took the card, then asked, "How likely is it?"

"Hard to say, but I don't think you need to worry. Even if they do call you in, you won't be considered a suspect. This is off the record, but I believe Bethany accused you to cause trouble, especially with that insulting description she gave of your anatomy."

I drove home, still not quite believing Bethany had gone so far to hurt me and Natalie. Hell, after this stunt, she'd be lucky if she kept her job—especially since I had every intention of calling George in the morning. I was willing to let her abuse of me slide, but she'd gone too far. I wasn't about to let her do it to someone else. Making the turn onto my street,

I pushed my ex-boss from my mind. I had more pleasant things to think about. Gina had already taken Natalie home and I couldn't wait to continue our day.

We could do a short scene. Maybe Natalie would enjoy some sensation play, or I could get out that bison hide flogger she liked so much. Thuddy with just a touch of sting, she always said it felt like a massage. Of course, having another Myrtle Beach night sounded good too. I had a feeling there were going to be several of those evenings in our near future and they didn't have to be on a Saturday.

My head already in dom space, I pulled into the driveway and frowned when I found Natalie's car gone. She didn't answer a text, and my call went straight to voicemail, so I tried Samantha.

When the call connected, I said, "Sorry to bother you again, but Natalie's car is gone. Is she with you and Gina?"

"No problem. I'm not home yet, so I'll have to get back to you in about half an hour."

"Thanks." I ended the call and went inside, detouring to the kitchen table where she'd left her last note. Nothing was there except the folder filled with paperwork, and a quick search of the house and yard gained me nothing except more questions.

"Where are you, baby girl?"

***

After waiting nearly three hours for Natalie to either come home or return my texts, I was torn between being furious and terrified for her safety. Fifty dollars' worth of sushi was in the fridge, delivered from a local Japanese restaurant. It would keep, but not for much longer.

My phone rested on the table, irritatingly silent. I considered texting Samantha and Gina again, but I'd already bothered them twice. Hell, I didn't even know who her friends were these days. I had a couple of numbers for her teaching colleagues, but those wouldn't help. Considering she'd been retired for better than three months, I didn't see her contacting any of them.

Not only did I not know her friends, I hadn't known she'd retired. Fuck, I was a shitty husband. Maybe I did know one friend though. Diving for my wallet, I dug through it in search of Charles's card, but came up empty. What had I done with it? Racing upstairs, I checked the pockets in my rented tuxedo.

"Thank fuck." I pulled the card from the pants pocket and went back downstairs. As I was reaching for my phone, the front door opened.

Her head lowered, Natalie walked in and stopped on the throw rug. Without speaking, she removed her sweater, followed by her dress and shoes, then knelt on the floor and laced her fingers behind her head. The steel collar she'd worn all weekend was the only thing left.

"Where have you been, baby? You didn't answer your phone, and I've been worried." Although I tried to keep my tone even and gentle, she flinched.

"I'm sorry, Master. I need to..." She choked out a breath, her shoulders shaking. "I need to tell you my truths."

I might still be upset with her, but I recognized her distress. "C'mon, baby," I murmured, helping her to her feet. "Truth telling only happens when you're sitting in my lap on the couch."

A tremulous smile danced across her face. "Is that a rule?"

"It is now." Putting an arm around her waist, I held her close as we walked into the living room. Once we were comfortably situated with her on my lap, I kissed her disheveled hair. "Okay, we're ready now."

"Are you mad at me?"

"No. Worried and upset you didn't answer my texts, yes." She shivered, making me reach for an afghan to cover her. "What happened?"

"I'm an idiot," she said after taking a deep breath. "I... Well, lots of reasons. In the police station, there were a few minutes when I actually wondered if you did what they said, but I knew it couldn't be true. And when I learned she'd been in our basement..."

My chest ached from the gut punch of hurt, but I needed her to confide in me more than I needed to rage about her lack of trust. Of course, the evidence alone had been damning enough to get us a visit from the police, so I couldn't blame her. Aside from that, we'd been out of touch with each other for too long.

"And you did leave me alone for the times they wanted to know about. I had no proof you were even still in the house."

"I watched you on the monitor all night," I said softly.

"I know. I mean, I figured, but I couldn't prove it. Anyway, Bethany being in our house got stuck in my head, and I felt so violated. It was like she tarnished everything that happened this weekend into something ugly."

Tears dripped to my shirt, and I hugged her close. "First off, you aren't an idiot. I think she must have snuck in when we had that barbecue a few years ago."

"Yeah." She looked up, smiling softly. "Let's just say my brain is an idiot. Anyway, I couldn't see you when I was so stupid confused about what I was feeling, so I drove into the city to see Martine."

"That's your therapist, right?" When she nodded, I said, "Wonder if she could sneak me in for a session. I'm feeling a little violated about Bethany being in our basement too."

A sweet smile crossed her lips and she laid her head on my shoulder. "She said your Myrtle Beach idea was brilliant."

"What else did you talk about?"

"She reminded me I couldn't control my feelings, but I can control how I react to them. So, I came home to tell you everything."

"Did talking to her make you feel better?"

"Yeah. I still have the same feelings, but she helps me put them in order so I can keep them straight. It's like…they're less overwhelming, and I can deal with them more logically."

"That's good." Tipping up her chin, I kissed her, then brushed a few tears from her cheeks. "I don't want you to stop seeing her, baby. You call for an appointment whenever you feel you need it, okay? And if you and she think it will be helpful, I'll come with you."

"Yes, Master." She went silent for several seconds, letting me enjoy the warmth of her curled in my lap. "May I ask you a question?"

"Of course. You don't need permission for that."

"What was the evidence that exonerated you?"

"They didn't tell you?"

"I didn't ask because I knew it wasn't you. I just… You know."

"Your brain got stupid?" I asked, teasing her gently.

"Yeah." She returned my grin. "I didn't need

to know because you couldn't have done what she accused."

"You knew I didn't do it, but you felt like I did, is that what I'm understanding?"

She sighed and looked away. "Well, when you put it that way… I'm really sorry, Henry. I don't know what was going through my head."

My upset faded. Although we'd have to discuss the way she disappeared, I was glad she had someone to talk to. Soon, hopefully, that person would be me, but we had to get back to that point in our relationship first.

"The only thing we need to talk about is how you went off without telling anyone where you were. I'm not going to control your daily life, but I want you to tell me where you're going. I'll do the same." Hugging her, I rested my chin on the top of her head. "Okay?"

"Yes, Master. I won't do it again."

"Good girl. No punishment this time because it wasn't a rule."

Her face fell, but she nodded her agreement. "Okay, Master."

"However, I might think of a new game so you don't forget," I added, remembering her inability to let go unless the slate was cleared between us.

"What kind of game?"

I tapped her nose. "We'll talk about it after supper. You wanted to know what the evidence was, right?"

Blinking, she straightened. "Oh, yes. What did they find?"

I cleared my throat and my face heated. "Apparently, Bethany took artistic license with her description of my anatomy."

"I don't understand."

"She said I had a smelly, uncircumcised micropenis. I might or might not have dropped trou in front of Detective Whalen."

Natalie

I choked, then suddenly I was laughing so hard I nearly fell off Henry's lap. It was so damned funny and I couldn't stop. Tears poured down my face and I coughed, hardly able to breathe. Although he still looked slightly embarrassed, he didn't seem offended.

Taking a deep breath, I flopped next to him on the couch and tried to calm down.

"What's so funny?"

"I'm just picturing Detective Whalen's face while you showed her your junk. She must have turned as red as a tomato."

"Actually, she was very professional about it. I'm sure I'm not the first person to wave his Johnson in front of her."

"What possessed you to do that?"

"They were talking about me having a medical exam. I decided to save everyone some time and effort." He helped me off the couch and looped a finger through the ring on my collar. "Come. Naughty girls need their spankings before supper."

My stomach swirled with a mixture of trepidation and excitement, and I had no idea which one would come out on top. "I thought you said you weren't going to punish me."

"I'm not," he replied, leading me to the basement steps. "I'm going to spank you because I want to."

He led me down the stairs, staying in front of me so I didn't fall. Instead of what used to be our normal routine—meaning the spanking bench—he put his hand in my hair and guided me to the couch.

"Don't you want me to pick something from the implement rack, Master?"

"No." He cupped my cheeks, tracing his thumbs over my cheekbones. "Do you remember how we used to be when we first started exploring D/s?"

"Yes." Closing my eyes, I smiled at the memory. Neither of us had much money for equipment back then, but we had big dreams and even bigger imaginations. We perverted the most innocuous household items into toys for play time, but Henry's favorite had always been his own hands.

"Good girl." He kissed me, his lips soft and gentle against mine, then sat down.

I didn't need an invitation, and was moving before he patted his knee. Some of our most meaningful, intimate encounters had started just like this.

He stroked my ass, his strong, callused palm sending a shiver up my spine. Henry always knew just how to touch me to set the stage for our scenes. Yet this wasn't so much a scene as a reconnection and reconciliation. My muscles relaxed until I felt like I was sinking into his lap and I matched my breathing to his soft exhalations.

"I'm ready, Master," I whispered.

"Let's get you warmed up."

Cool air brushed across my backside when he lifted his hand and I clenched instinctively. I knew better, but I still did it.

SLAP.

I let out a sharp gasp at both the sting and the sound, but my body relaxed again. "One."

"Don't count, baby. I'll be spanking you until I'm done."

Perfect.

His hand rose and fell in a measured, steady rhythm as he roasted my butt, the sting morphing into heat. God, it felt so good. It was just like it used to be between us. A spanking, just because he thought I needed one, without any expectation, no planned scene or big production. Just my husband and his firm hand. Tears pricked my eyes, although I couldn't say what I was crying over because I wasn't unhappy. Quite the opposite, in fact. His hand on my ass was better than any drug for sending me flying. I didn't need our playroom or anything from our toy collection. Just him, his warmth and scent, and his touch.

I couldn't imagine a better way to spend a Sunday evening.

He petted me, sending tingles between my thighs. "Feel good, baby?"

"Mmmm." Stretching, I parted my thighs to invite his touch between my legs. "Uh huh."

"Looks like my baby girl is needy," he murmured, stroking my wet pussy.

I arched my back, exposing my core for more of his touch. "Are you going to do something about it?"

"Do you think I should?"

"I… Oh, fuck me."

My words burst free on a low moan as he pushed two fingers inside me and curled them down. His thumb circled my clit and I shut my eyes, desperate to hold back the climax surging through my belly.

Without warning, he removed his hand and I whined, but didn't say anything. Henry was a sadist. I loved that about him, but there wasn't any arguing with him if he wanted to edge me. Then again, this was a new dynamic. Maybe I could argue just a little.

"Master, please," I begged, lifting my chest off the

couch to see his face, then sighed in disappointment at his stern gaze.

"After supper, if you're a good girl," he countered, helping me kneel between his legs. "But you'll have to be a very good girl."

Reaching for his fly, he unbuttoned his pants and revealed his thick cock. I fucking blushed at his naughty wink. How the hell had my own husband made me blush at my age? My mouth watered for a taste of his gorgeous erection and I leaned forward.

"I can be a very good girl," I breathed, brushing my lips over the swollen crown.

"Yes, you can." His voice guttural and harsh with need, he twisted a hand in my hair, tugging just hard enough to send a fresh punch of arousal into my core. "Put your hands behind your back and show me."

I folded my arms behind me, then lowered myself to him and licked a circle around the plump head of his shaft before pulling him into my mouth. The scent and taste of him flooded my senses, thrilling me with another sudden wave of need. The platinum ring in the tip of his erection slid against my tongue and I took a moment to play with it.

"Look at me," he ordered hoarsely.

I obeyed, meeting his fierce brown gaze. Jaw tight, he kept his eyes locked on mine as I made love to him with my mouth, telling him without words how much he meant to me. I relaxed my throat, hoping I hadn't forgotten how to suck his piercing past my gag reflex. It had been way too long.

The position was awkward, and I couldn't get the right angle to make it work. I tried my best though, wanting nothing more than to listen to his increasingly desperate moans. I promised myself I'd practice later.

He swelled in my mouth, his breath rasping as he tried to pull me away. "Baby, I'm gonna come," he warned.

Since when did he warn me about climaxes? I let my hands fall, then brought them up and dug my nails into his thighs. Instead of letting him go, I took him as deeply as I could, desperate to taste him. I needed him more than I needed to breathe.

It didn't matter that he hadn't let me come. All I needed was to be on my knees before him. He would make everything okay. I was ready for the salty liquid heat filling my mouth to flow down my throat, but I wanted more. Pulling back, I held him in one hand and allowed the last few drops to land on my face and chest.

"God, Natalie." He leaned forward and helped me up, then pulled me back into his lap.

"Does that mean I'm a good girl?" I asked, snuggling against his chest. My butt was already reminding me I'd been spanked and warm pulses were still making my core clench with need.

"You're a very good girl, baby."

CHAPTER SEVENTEEN

Henry

I tried to steady my breathing, but damn, Natalie knocked me for a loop. The blowjob wasn't as amazing as having her back in my arms where she belonged, and I started making plans for the sensual play scene she'd more than earned.

I'd never forget how close I'd come to losing her.

"How are you feeling?" I asked.

"Good, but I'm really hungry," she replied. "Do you want me to heat up a few of those meals or call for takeout?"

"I have the perfect thing for a hungry submissive," I said, helping her up after I zipped my pants. "I got a party platter from Kyoto Grill."

"Sounds delicious." She followed me across the basement, then helped with the heavy tray.

Sitting, I tore the paper from a pair of disposable chopsticks and used them to gesture at the floor between my feet. "Don't forget your cushion, baby."

Her eyes darkened and she licked her lips, then retrieved the pillow and dropped it between my feet. Taking her hand, I helped her kneel.

"I remember this." She shifted her weight, easing her thighs apart to reveal the piercing at the apex of her sex, then closed her eyes. "You used to feed me before scenes all the time."

"After supper, I was thinking we might do some sensation play."

She accepted a salmon roll. "Master, may I ask you a question?"

"What do you need, baby?"

She bit her lip, but looked up to meet my gaze. "I want to clean the basement from top to bottom. It smells, and I need to erase Bethany from my house and my memory."

"Come on." I stood and helped her to her feet, then grabbed the tray to carry it upstairs. "We'll repaint and lay carpet. It won't look anything like Bethany saw, and I'll have security cameras installed to make sure she never comes back.

"Do you think she will?"

"No, but I'd have said she wouldn't accuse an innocent man of assault either. Grab a bottle of wine from the fridge and we'll eat upstairs."

I let her go up the stairs ahead of me, mostly so I could watch her butt, and grabbed a cushion from one of the kitchen chairs. She knelt between my knees again, resting her hands on her thighs as I poured a glass of wine and gave her a sip.

"What do you want to do tomorrow?" she asked, accepting another sushi roll.

"We'll think about that tomorrow," I replied. I had a honey-do list a mile long, but I wasn't about to bring it up.

"All right, Scarlett," she said, giving me an amused smile.

"Smartass. What do you want to do?"

"Stay in bed and make love all day." She set the wine aside and reached up to kiss me. "We're retired, remember? We can do whatever we want."

"Excellent point." I fed her another piece of sushi. "You know what I'd like to do tonight though?"

Swallowing, she shook her head. "What's that?"

"Slave Tag."

Blinking, she got to her feet and backed away. "But it's dark!"

"So?" I stood and reached in the coat closet for my old paintball rifle. "Gives you a sporting chance, right?"

Her eyes widened and she peered around as if looking for an escape. "Aren't we a little old for this, Henry?"

I had no intention of shooting her with a paintball. They stung like crazy on bare skin. If I was sure I'd hit her in a well-cushioned area and her face was protected, I might consider it, but not after dark and certainly not while I didn't know which way she'd duck. As far as I could tell, the thing wasn't even loaded. She didn't know any of that. "As often as you work out, are you telling me you don't think you can escape? Such a pity."

A flare of challenge lit in her eyes and she trotted up the stairs, returning moments later with her sneakers. "Are you sure about this?" she asked, lacing her shoes. "It's getting late."

Opening the back door with a flourish, I gestured outside. "You have a one-minute head start. If I can't catch you within five minutes, you get a reward."

Natalie sidled through the door, her eyes narrowed with wariness. "What happens if you catch me?"

"You cut a switch for me and bend yourself over the deck rail for punishment."

"Henry, I..." She bit her lip and peered at me from under her lashes. "It's just like old times."

I cocked the paintball gun, then pointed out the door with the muzzle. "Run, baby girl."

Letting out a soft squeak, she vanished into the darkness. I put the gun back into the closet and sauntered out after her.

Natalie

My belly swirled with a delicious mixture of fear and arousal as I dashed down the back steps. A few sprinkles of rain brushed across my shoulders, the chilled moisture seeming to erupt into steam on contact with my skin.

As usual, I had no idea if I wanted to escape or be caught. Despite the distance between us during the bad years, our chemistry was every bit as incendiary as before.

I couldn't hear a damned thing except the pounding of my heart beating in time with my footfalls on the slick grass, and the scent of rain-drenched roses filled the air in a fragrantly heady cloud. I felt...good. Like everything that had worried me over the years disappeared and I was newly born into something else.

Something fresh and wild.

Rose thorns scratched at me, but I imagined Henry could smell the faint traces of blood I left behind, like an animal from a paranormal romance novel. Unrealistic, but the fantasy added spice to the chase. Soundlessly, I slipped through the gate leading to the rest of the property, intending to make him work for it.

"Olly olly oxen free," he called.

He didn't mean it. Henry would do exactly as he promised if he caught me. Darting to the side, I jumped to catch the low branches of an oak tree and grunted with exertion as I hauled myself up into the concealing vegetation. I was getting too old to be climbing trees and playing Slave Tag with my husband, but I'd take it while I could. The bark was rough against my bare ass, but I held myself as still as I could and let my calves dangle over the tree limb.

If it was daylight, I'd see faint spots of brown on the leaves heralding fall, but for now, there was plenty of foliage to hide me. Henry almost never looked up.

His face creased with worry, he passed under me as a flash of lightning illuminated the garden. "Baby, our game is called on account of rain. Let's go inside."

I didn't bother to hide a smile. Henry might shove a piece of ginger in my ass and cane me until I sobbed and begged for mercy, but he wasn't about to let me get caught in a little storm. Doms were funny creatures.

As I shifted my weight to climb down, something grabbed my ankle and pulled, yanking me off balance. Screeching, I tumbled down, landing in Henry's arms. He grunted and dropped to his knees, sending us both sprawling.

I was laughing too hard to speak and flopped to my back, letting the rain bathe my face.

"That looked better in my imagination," Henry confessed, making me laugh even harder.

"Are you okay?" I asked, my giggles tapering off. We were both soaked to the skin and sitting in mud.

"I'm fine. Are you?"

"Yeah. You caught me." I straddled his waist, biting back a gasp as my pussy rubbed against his hard bulge. "I guess I better cut that switch."

I climbed off his lap and he handed me a small pair of garden shears, then leaned forward to kiss my forehead. "You have two minutes, but make sure it's a good one. You know what will happen if it breaks."

The sudden surge of arousal made my knees

tremble as I made my way to a thicket of willow saplings. Thin and flexible, they'd be perfect for what we needed. Taking my time, I cut one about three feet long and the diameter of a pencil at its base.

When I returned, he took the switch and tsked at me. "Naughty girl. You've earned yourself some extra licks for dawdling."

"I'm sorry, Master. Forgive me?"

"Should I?" he asked, hooking a finger through the ring on my collar. "Seems to me you want that extra switching."

His voice deepened, sending a thrill down my spine. Henry and I were yin and yang. Sadist and masochist. The missing piece of my heart. How had I survived so long without submitting to my master? I should have… Nope, I wasn't going there. We'd already talked things out, and it was time to move forward.

"It will be as many as you think I need, Master."

His eyes softened and he traced a finger down the line of my jaw. "I love you, baby. Hands behind your head, and walk in front of me to the deck."

"I love you back, Master." I obeyed, my core clenching as he tapped my backside with the switch. When we reached the deck, he grabbed a cushion from a chair and laid it over the railing. I bent over, my chest hitting a canvas pillow instead of hard wood.

The rain soaked my hair, sending it to hang in my face like a shimmery silver curtain. I smelled ozone mixed with musk from his skin and I inhaled, drawing the fragrance deep into my lungs like I was breathing the tempest.

"Good girl. Let's get you warmed up." Petting me, he leaned down and kissed the back of my neck as the rain chilled, making my skin pebble with gooseflesh. He rubbed my backside firmly, bringing blood to the surface. The switching was going to hurt and I couldn't wait.

The switch whistled, then lit up a streak of fiery sensation across the backs of my thighs.

"Oh, God."

"Feet apart, baby. Point your toes in."

I obeyed and my core spasmed as another stroke fell, then a third and a fourth. The position made it harder for me to clench my muscles—a fact Henry always took advantage of. The rain pummeled my back like liquid trails from a flogger, and I arched, exposing every inch of skin I could to the scorching flare of heat from the switch combined with icy water.

"Look at you," Henry said, drawing the switch down the middle of my back. "I bet you're ready to be fucked, aren't you?"

"Please," I begged, desperate to stay still when he dragged the tip of the switch up my inner thigh and prodded at my clit. If he wasn't very careful, I was going to come without permission.

"I love to hear you say please, Natalie." He replaced the switch with his fingers and I bit back a cry of pleasure. "I especially love to say no after you beg. Your tears make my dick hard."

Whimpering, I arched my back, making sure Henry saw the wetness coating my pussy. "I need you," I whispered.

Crouching, he cupped my chin, making me face him. "I need you more,' he croaked, moisture that might or might not have been rain dripping from his eyelashes. "I need a color first, baby."

"Green, Master. I'm always green with you."

He pushed his hand into my hair and tugged until

I straightened, pulling hard enough to skirt the razor edge between delight and agony. I wanted to balance there forever like a high-wire dancer. My nipples, already stiffened with cold, pricked and pebbled, begging for the sweet torture Henry delivered with such precise skill.

He set the base of the switch against my throat, forcing my chin up. "Will you cry for me if I fuck your ass, little slave?"

"I'll cry if you don't," I replied in a hoarse whisper, swallowing against the pressure on my neck.

"Good girl." He laid a hand on my shoulder, encouraging me to my knees. Unbuttoning his pants, he freed his thick cock, already hard and dripping precum for me, then brushed it against my lips. "Suck, Natalie. Get me wet."

The captive bead on his piercing brushed against my lower lip before coming to rest on my tongue. I wanted to play with it like I used to, but when Henry's fist tightened in my hair once more, I got my mind on business and pulled his thick hardness into my mouth, slicking him with spit.

I loved the sharp pinch of humiliation of this specific act. He'd always say my spit would be the only lube I'd get, but I knew better. My husband wouldn't take me dry, but the threat made me so freaking hot. Still, it was a point of honor for me to make sure he was wet enough. I circled the plush head, sucking the sweetness of precum down my throat as he twitched in my mouth and groaned, his hips bucking.

Without warning, he pulled me to my feet, using my hair as a leash, and led me to the cushioned daybed under the porch overhang. "On your knees, baby. Ass in the air," he ordered.

My pussy dripped as I obeyed, spreading my knees wide. He pushed my shoulders down, then knelt behind me and spread my buttocks wide. Instead of pushing inside me, he teased my soaking wet flesh, rubbing the crown of his cock against my clit. Slowly, he eased into my slick channel and I hissed in pleasure, clenching around the heated intrusion.

"Oh, baby," he crooned, squeezing my hip. "You think you're going to come with my dick in that sweet pussy?"

"No, Master." I choked on the words as his piercing scraped across my g-spot. I wanted to though. It would be worth the punishment.

I almost cried when he pulled out, but he positioned himself at my back entrance and patiently eased his way into me. He filled me to the brim and stilled. I bucked against him, desperate for more, needing him to move inside me.

He slapped my hip hard, making me cry out. "Fuck me, pet. Rock that sweet ass against me, and if you do a good job, I'll let you come."

God, yes. Pushing my hips back, I obeyed, letting him fill me, his heavy balls slapping at my clit on each stroke. It wasn't nearly enough to make me come and he knew it, the sadistic bastard. The sensual tease was excruciatingly divine, sweet temptation. I was his willing slave, drawn to the honeyed anguish only he could deliver.

"That's my good girl," he murmured, pulling me against his chest as he sat back on his heels. My knees were splayed wide over his thighs, exposing my pussy to his touch. "Keep fucking me and squeeze that tight ass around my dick."

"Please." I panted the word, barely able to speak as I rose and fell, using my body weight to force him deep into my ass.

"Harder, baby. You can do better than that." His hand fell against my exposed pussy, the slap ringing over the sound of thunder from the storm. "I bet you'll come if I keep slapping that beautiful cunt."

"Oh, fuck."

He wrapped an arm around me and squeezed my nipple between two fingers, sending pulsing electricity to my clit as he spanked my pussy. His warm breath feathered across the back of my neck, making me shudder. "Aw, baby. An f-bomb? Wonder how many cane strokes you'll get before I let you come."

"Henry, please!" I screeched over the pounding thunder, my voice cracking.

He grunted and dug his fingers into the skin over my hipbone. "Fuck me like you mean it and we'll come together."

Instead of making me do all the work, he helped me, his hand on my hip guiding me as he surged into me. It felt so damned good. My body sang with prickles of pain. Cold rain poured down, unable to douse the fire building between us.

"Please, please, please," I begged.

"On three, baby girl," he choked out, his cock swelling inside me.

He counted too slowly. My vision blurred and I shuddered from the force of the sensual conflagration welling inside me. I couldn't breathe or speak as a ferocious climax surged.

"Now!" Henry gave my pussy one last stinging slap, then pinched my clit.

My guts seized and I let out a breathless scream as a massive orgasm knocked my world off its axis and stole my wits along with my consciousness.

CHAPTER EIGHTEEN

Henry

Holy. Shit.

I had zero words for what happened between us. It was pouring rain. Natalie was almost insensate and sprawled across my chest. My back ached from holding her up almost as much as my balls did. The storm still raged and I would have given anything to have the strength to carry her inside. Neither one of us needed to be out in this weather. Groaning, I eased her off my lap and tried to stand. My knees wobbled, but I managed it.

"Hey, sweetie," I said, helping her sit up, "We need to get inside."

She blinked, her blue eyes wide and owlish with dilated pupils. "Okay," she slurred, her words slow and deliberate. "I think you fucked me stupid."

"I could say the same thing about you," I replied, hiding a smile as I helped her stand. "Tonight's aftercare is brought to you by the words *shower* and *unconscious*."

"And the number twelve," she added, trudging inside ahead of me.

"Twelve?" I followed her up the stairs, scowling at the scratches on her arms and legs. I'd need to take care of those before we could go to bed.

"The hours of sleep I better have before anyone bothers me." She walked straight into the shower stall, stopping to turn on the taps.

I followed her in, making sure the water was warm enough. "Sounds like a plan, but I need to make sure all those scratches are cleaned up."

"Funny," she replied, dropping to her knees. "I need to make sure something else is clean."

"Natalie," I warned, lifting her up. "What did I tell you about aftercare?"

She bit her lip and nodded. "Sorry, Master."

"Good girl." Grabbing the soap, I scrubbed her from head to toe, paying extra attention to her abrasions. Nothing was deep enough to require a bandage, thank goodness. I hurried through my own shower, letting her lean against the tile, her eyes half closed as she watched me bathe.

We dried each other and fell into bed. I was almost too tired to spoon, but I didn't want her out of my reach. "I love you, baby girl. Sorry about the crappy aftercare."

"You give exactly the aftercare I need, Master." She snuggled under the covers, tucking her head against my arm. "I love you back."

She fell asleep almost immediately. I stayed awake longer than I should have, simply enjoying having her in my arms. I'd come too close to losing her to waste a single moment.

***

Praying Natalie was still asleep, I crept into our bedroom, the product of my early morning errand burning a hole in my jacket pocket. Thankfully, she was sprawled on her belly, her eyes closed. Her hair was a tangled mess poking up from under the covers, but she'd never looked more beautiful. She grunted in her sleep and rolled over, her hand moving to my side of the bed. Something ached deep in my chest at the gesture. Even in sleep, she reached for me.

After hanging up the garment bags containing surprises for later, I pushed the sheet aside to check the scratches on her arm. Although still somewhat pink, they'd heal up in no time. Leaning close, I kissed her shoulder. Last night had been beyond exciting. I couldn't remember having such an amazing scene with her.

I crept downstairs to make a pot of coffee and finish making plans. Tapping the number from Charles's embossed business card into my phone, I waited impatiently for it to connect.

"Benson Galleries," an androgynous voice said.

"Good morning. This is Henry Mercer, and I'd like to speak to Charles Benson, please."

"This is Charles. As a matter of fact, I was just thinking of you and my dear Natalie. How is she?"

"She's still asleep," I replied, slipping outside so Natalie didn't hear me. "I'm calling to ask a favor. Do you have a key to her apartment?"

"I rather think I've already given you a favor for not calling the cops this morning when I happened to review my security camera footage. Tell me why I shouldn't call them, Mr. Mercer."

I winced and walked further into Natalie's rose garden. As much as his questions irritated me, I was glad she had a friend looking out for her. "I'm... Yeah, I have no excuse for that, and I'm thanking all the gods I can think of that Natalie forgave me."

Charles was silent for several seconds, then said, "You must love her very much to take such a risk."

"More than my own life. I had to fix what I broke between us." I paused a moment, then added, "I'll have her call you when she wakes up so you can confirm what I said."

"And did you fix what was broken?"

"I hope so. That leads me to the favor I wanted to ask."

"What do you need from me?"

When I told him, he laughed softly and said, "I was always a sucker for a good love story. I'll drop everything off in a few hours."

After thanking him, I ended the call and crept inside, then poured fresh coffee into a carafe and arranged pastries from her favorite bakery on a tray. Before going upstairs, I detoured to the basement for a heavier cane and a spray bottle filled with iced water, along with another carved ginger plug. With luck, I'd be needing them.

Keeping my steps quiet, I carried our breakfast up to our room and set it on the nightstand.

"I smell coffee," she muttered sleepily from her nest under the covers. "Is there ibuprofen? I feel like someone's been beating me with a stick."

"Well…"

I bit back a grin as an irritable blue eye peered at me from behind a curtain of silver hair. "You gonna go there this early in the morning?"

"It's almost noon." I poured her a cup, then got a bottle of pain reliever from the bathroom and handed her two.

She swallowed them with a sip of coffee, then laid back down and pulled the sheet over her head. "Too early."

"Time to get up, sleepyhead." I pulled the sheet down, revealing the curve of her breast, then lowered my head to a budding nipple and sucked it into my mouth.

Letting out a soft moan, she arched her back and sank her hands into my hair. "I'm not complaining, but I thought we had to get up."

"Later. Hands over your head." When she opened her mouth to protest, I pinched her damp nipple, making her hiss out a breath.

Her eyes dilated and a pink blush suffused her cheeks as she obeyed me. "Yes, Master."

"Good girl." Still fully dressed, I crawled between her legs, my shoulders wedging her thighs apart. Lowering my head, I inhaled her musky perfume, then swirled my tongue around her clit piercing.

She bucked and cried out, giving me better access to her sweet pussy. Without letting up on her clit, I pushed two fingers inside her and curled them to tease her g-spot.

"Master, please!"

"Not yet. Hold it in for me, baby." Her thighs shook as I slowly fucked her with my fingers, driving her closer to the edge. "If you come without permission, I'll have to punish you."

"Fuck. I... Henry, please!" She thrashed under me, sweat slicking her beautiful body as her pussy clenched around my fingers.

My dick hardened to the point of pain, but I ignored it in favor of today's game. Turning my hand, I eased a thumb into her ass and kept sucking her clit.

"Oh, God. I... Oh, my God." Without warning, she exploded, screaming my name.

Giving her clit one last swipe with my tongue, I rose up and kissed her, letting her taste herself on my lips. "Naughty girl," I chided softly. "Did I give you permission to come?"

Sadist that I was, I'd set her up for failure. My sweet wife had many surprises waiting for her.

Her muscles going lax, she let her head fall backward to the pillow, a wry smile crossing her lips.

"Asshole," she muttered, turning over to expose her cute round backside.

"Up on your knees, baby. How many should I give you?" I asked, grabbing the cane.

She obeyed, getting up on all fours. "It will be as many as you think I need, Master."

I nudged her shoulders down gently until she rested her head on the pillow and her ass was fully exposed. The lines from her previous punishments were almost gone, and I was itching to replace them with new ones. Her slim, muscular thighs were going to get my attention today. She'd be sitting on them most of the afternoon.

"Good girl. Don't bother to count." Backing up, I lifted the cane and brought it down across the lower curve of her ass. A red line blossomed almost immediately over both globes of her buttocks and I traced it with the tip of the cane before laying down a second just below the first.

She whimpered, her bottom clenching and releasing as she steadied her position. Wetness glistened on the delicate folds of her pussy and my mouth watered. Instead of going in for another taste, I stroked her damp flesh with the cane.

"Needy little girl," I murmured. "Do you like that?"

She sucked in a breath, then exhaled. "You know I do, Master."

Natalie was one of those very rare submissives who could climax from a caning. On the surface, we sounded like a perfect pairing—sadist and masochist—but it required a great deal of focus and balance. I didn't want her to come every time I caned her. Sometimes, I just wanted to give her the pain.

Today would be a test of all my skills, her

resilience, and the strength of our love for each other.

Natalie

The two lines Henry laid across the tops of my thighs burned like fire, sending pulses of heat into my core with every beat of my heart. I had a love/hate relationship with his collection of birches, rods, and canes. He'd spent years perfecting his craft, starting with a pillow coated in baby powder, then a ballistic gel model of my backside, and finally on…me.

Leave it to an engineer to get carried away with his experiments when all I wanted was a thorough ass-beating. I'd say one thing for him though. He never failed to get me off—when he wanted to.

Sadly, that almost never happened. Fucking sadist.

He laid three lines in quick succession down my thighs, allowing the heavy rattan cane to wrap slightly. That could be dangerous, but after so many years of practice, he never missed his placement. The strike went exactly where he wanted it and I tightened my muscles, needing to feel the extra sting.

I almost smiled when he slapped my ass. "No clenching to make it hurt more, baby," he warned. "You know better."

"Sorry, I can't help it." I let out a breath and tried to relax. He always stopped if he thought I was enjoying it too much.

"Good thing I have something to remind you."

"Asshole," I hissed, knowing he'd set me up. Yet it was exactly what I needed. Pressing my thighs together, I attempted to ease the growing ache between my legs, but it just made things worse.

He laid a gentle hand on my hip, and I felt something cold prod at my back opening a second before the sharp fragrance of ginger permeated the air. The carved root slid easily inside me and I closed my eyes, waiting for it to light me on fire.

"Such language," he murmured, laying two more stripes across my thighs. The cool chill of ice water made me shiver as he sprayed me down.

Fuck. This wasn't punishment, not when a thorough, sensual caning was one of my favorite things in the world. The heavier cane he was using was more thuddy than stingy, sending sensation deep into my muscles. In contrast to the lighter Delrin, which left a sharp, unsatisfying sting, the decadent, throbbing ache from the heavy cane would stick around for hours.

The ginger added its own brand of torment, the burning tease making my pussy clench with want. I wanted to kick myself for not trying it before. Hell, I'd plant a whole flowerbed with the stuff, and even bring some inside for winter. I could definitely see myself begging for it.

Henry would refuse with a wicked smirk on his face while he denied my body's desire for sweet agony. Fucking sadist.

"Naughty girl," he murmured, laying two more stripes down a few inches above my knees. "I'm not a fucking sadist, I'm your husband."

"You're both," I choked out, realizing I'd said it out loud. God, the fantastically perfect pain he delivered with just a few strokes of an implement.

The dichotomy of him, tender and caring, cruel and biting while he delivered unfathomable suffering to me, was my Waterloo. My *raison d'être*.

"Should I get a ruler?" he asked, tracing one of the lines with the tip of his cane. "I'm out of practice. I think I might be off a few millimeters."

God, I was going to kill him. I was so close to release. Just one more would send me over the edge into bliss. Instead of giving me what I needed, he stroked my ass with a gentle hand, then removed the ginger. I wanted to scream, but he'd like it too much.

"Fuck, Henry," I muttered, lifting my hips into his touch. "I'm going to boil you in your own pudding."

"F-bombs aren't going to get you what you want this time, baby," he murmured, helping me sit on the bed. I hissed with pleasure when the cool sheets hit my thighs and my core ached with need.

"Asshole." I reached for the coffee he'd poured for me and took a deep, restorative sip. "Now that I'm awake, what are we doing today?"

"I'm glad you asked," he replied, unzipping a garment bag hung on the closet door. "We're going to take a little trip, but you need to eat first."

I grabbed a cheese Danish from the tray and nibbled at the tender pastry. One look at his face convinced me not to ask where we were going. He wasn't going to tell me. I was surprisingly okay with that. The last time he took me somewhere for a surprise, it was to The Castle.

That would be the perfect place for us, and I'd be able to talk to Master Marshall in person about commissioning some of my art. Unfortunately, I didn't see Henry scoring a room for us on such short notice.

When I finished my Danish, I stood and stretched, loving the ache blossoming across the backs of my thighs, then went to clean up. I hurried through a quick shower and exited the bathroom, excited to see what Henry planned.

He reached into the garment bag and pulled out a black sheath dress and a pair of black Louboutin stilettos. I resisted the urge to coo over the gorgeous pumps. I was such a shoe whore. "Where are we going?"

"It's a surprise." Pulling out a small hex key, he removed the steel training collar, leaving my neck painfully bare.

"Henry…"

He popped my ass with the flat of his hand. "Get dressed, baby girl. I know I'm not supposed to pick out your clothes, but this is a special occasion."

I laughed helplessly and shook my head, taking the dress from him. "Yes, Master. It's not like I have anything else here to choose from anyway."

There weren't any panties, but there was a decadent black lace push-up bra and silk thigh-high stockings. Yum. Sitting on the bed, he crossed his arms across his chest and watched me dress, waiting patiently while I slapped a little makeup on from the stash in my purse and pinned my hair into a twist.

He looked amazing in faded jeans and a white dress shirt, the sleeves rolled back to reveal muscular arms. There was just something about a man's arms exposed under a dress shirt. So freaking sexy. Laying a hand on my hip, he escorted me outside and into his car.

The only thing I had was my purse, keys, and phone. I opened my mouth to ask once more where we were going, then looked at him out of the corner of my eye as he backed out of our driveway. He wasn't smiling, but his face was relaxed. At peace in a way I hadn't seen in years. Pressing my lips together, I smiled and he squeezed my fingers when I took his hand.

An hour later, he took the exit ramp to the airport and parked, then hustled me into the terminal with two carry-on bags.

"Henry," I said, trying to slow him down. "I don't have my passport. And where did this suitcase come from?"

"I asked Charles to pack for you, and you don't need a passport." He tugged on my hand. "Come on. We're going to miss our flight."

Holy shit. Henry didn't use the restroom without a plan of attack. It was unfathomable for him to take a trip requiring air travel without a ten-page itinerary.

I decided I didn't care.

We made it through security without issue, and he hustled me into a family restroom on the other side of the scanners, just across the concourse from a Starbucks.

"You're mine now, Natalie Kane," he murmured, pulling me into a deep kiss.

"Natalie Mercer." I made myself let go of his belt loops, then touched my swollen lips.

"I kidnapped Natalie Kane," he countered, his voice deepening into the raspy tone that always made me drip with arousal. He set his bag on the baby changing table and the sound of the zipper echoed. "You'll have to earn the Mercer name. Go ahead and use the facilities. You won't have a chance for a while."

I did as he asked, thankful he was polite enough to turn his back. After almost twenty years together, we didn't have that many secrets left, but it was still a nice gesture.

When I finished washing up, he said, "Bend over and grab your ankles."

Wherever we were going, this was the start of a scene and it wouldn't stop until I was begging for mercy. There was no point in arguing with him.

The only way I'd get out of this would be to drop a safeword. Yet if I did, I'd lose out on what he planned.

Boo hiss.

I obeyed, sliding my hands down the silk stockings until they reached my ankles.

He stroked my bare ass with a gentle fingertip, then spread my buttocks apart. Something cold and hard touched my asshole and I let out a breath, knowing I was about to get plugged.

"Good girl," he murmured, easing the toy into me. "Almost there." He seated the plug and helped me stand, then washed his hands and pulled a coil of boiled hemp rope from his bag.

"What's that for?" I asked suspiciously. Rope wasn't something we played with very often, but he was a passable rigger when the occasion called for it.

The end of the rope fell free as he doubled it, then wrapped it around my waist. "Just something to make sure we don't have any accidents. Hold your dress up a little more, please."

Within minutes, he had me trussed into a makeshift chastity belt complete with a knot centered over my clit. Knees wobbling, I straightened and caught my breath as the knot did all sorts of naughty things to my girly bits. The twin strands of rope centered between my labia didn't help. Worse, he'd used warming lube on the plug. The sensation wasn't as powerful as ginger, but still made my insides tingle.

"Dammit, Henry!" The thought of sitting on a plane like this made me quiver with need, and I couldn't deny the excitement from his game. "Are you serious?"

"Yep." Grinning at me, he tugged my dress into place, then zipped his suitcase. "Ready to go?"

CHAPTER NINETEEN

Henry

I let Natalie exit the bathroom first, trying to hide a grin at her awkward gait. The rope harness keeping the plug where it belonged, combined with the high heels made her ass sway enticingly. I almost hauled her back into the bathroom when I saw several men watch her as we passed by. There were even a few women giving her speculative gazes.

Ray's offhand complaint about other men looking at Ally like they wanted to fuck her made a lot more sense now. Natalie was a bit of an exhibitionist, and I used to be comfortable with other people seeing her body, but now... Yeah, not so much.

"Hoist with his own petard," I muttered.

"What was that?" she asked, slowing to look at me curiously.

"Nothing. Just talking to myself." Pointing ahead, I added, "There's our gate."

Her steps slowed, then stopped as she stared at the destination below our flight number. "Reno. Oh, my God. That's three..." Her eyes widened and she licked her lips, then shook her head. "We're going to Lake Tahoe, aren't we?"

"It's the same cottage where we spent our honeymoon," I murmured, guiding her to the podium when our boarding group was called. "Three hours in a plane seat with your thighs aching from a caning. Every time you move, that rope will rub against you and—"

Shuddering, she closed her eyes. "Oh, God."

I let her go ahead of me as we boarded, wanting her to have the window seat. Passengers slowly filled the plane and I watched with amusement while Natalie tried to bite back faint whines whenever she moved.

"Poor baby," I murmured. "It must be so hard to sit there with a plug in your ass, knowing you won't get relief for hours."

In a whisper so soft I could barely hear it, she said, "Fucking sadist."

"You realize how long it will be until I can punish you for the f-bombs, right? It's just going to keep getting bigger."

"Worth it. I think I'm going to start calling you FS instead of Master."

The plane lifted off the ground and I barked out a laugh. "Fair enough. It's even something you can use when we visit your parents." Leaning toward her, I cupped her cheek. "Don't forget, honey. You can safeword at any time. The bathroom is a few rows ahead, and I put the knot in front so you can get out of the harness by yourself."

She smiled faintly and brushed her lips over mine. "I know. I'm just… Nervous, I guess. We haven't played in public in ages."

The flight attendant walked down the aisle taking drink orders. When he reached us, I said, "Could we have two mimosas and a blanket for my wife? She's cold."

Nodding, he hurried away, then returned with our drinks and a folded blanket. Setting the drinks aside, I lifted the armrest between us and covered her, pulling the blanket over myself as well.

"What are you up to?" she asked. "I wasn't cold."

"Hmm." I rested a hand on her knee, then slowly pushed her skirt up. "You've been shivering, so I just assumed you were chilly."

"No, I…" Her eyes fell shut and she whimpered when my fingers found her wet heat and rubbed the knot over her clit. Safely hidden under the blanket, no one would see what I was doing.

"Please, don't edge me," she begged, a sparkling tear balanced on her long lashes. "I can't do it for three hours."

"Oh, baby. You know those pretty tears make my cock hard." I traced a finger down her elegant throat and kissed her gently. "I'm not going to edge you at all."

"Thank you, Master." She let out a sigh of relief and closed her eyes when I found her piercing.

"All you have to do is be very quiet."

"Oh, fuck me."

Natalie

By the time we landed in Reno-Tahoe, I was a boneless, dripping puddle of wrung out goo from the uncountable number of orgasms Henry had given me on the plane. It was all I could do to stumble next to him toward baggage claim and the exits. I barely had the strength to pull my own suitcase behind me, but he kept a firm arm wrapped around my waist, helping me walk a straight line.

"Do you need the restroom, baby?" he asked, turning me toward the appropriate door.

"Yes, Master." When he nodded, I trudged inside and went into a stall, then took care of business without losing the butt plug or messing up Henry's rope work. After washing up, I turned and walked into a wall. God help me, I stood there wondering where the door was until Henry peeked inside and came to get me.

"Martine will not be happy with me."

"You need aftercare," he replied, guiding me toward a man holding a sign bearing our last name. "You'll get it the minute we're in the limo."

We followed the chauffer to a black town car and climbed into the back seat. Henry shoved a piece of chocolate into my mouth, then handed me a bottle of sports drink. I swallowed and took a sip from the bottle, feeling the sugar knock my brain back online.

"Fancy." I blinked and looked around. "Why aren't we getting on I-80? Wasn't the rental in Polaris?"

"We're going somewhere else first. In fact…" He paused and wrapped a cloth blindfold around my head. "It's a surprise."

I almost protested the blindfold, but I kept my mouth shut when he pulled me into his lap and stroked my back. "Where are we going?"

"Not telling, but it's about another ten minutes."

"What will we be doing there?"

He laid a hand on my face, then kissed me, taking his time until I was gasping and a renewed surge of need welled in my pussy. As I started to beg for his touch again, the limousine stopped and the driver's door opened then closed.

I jerked away and straightened my skirt, but knew Henry wouldn't let me take off the blindfold.

"Watch your step," he murmured, helping me walk over a hard surface as the sun heated my shoulders. A door opened and the chill of air conditioning made my bare arms pebble with gooseflesh.

"Where are we?" I asked, reaching up for the

blindfold.

A warm hand pulled my fingers away from the cloth. "Soon, baby. Be patient just a bit longer. First, we need to get you changed."

"Changed into what?" He lifted my skirt, but I held it down, tugging it free. "Who's here?"

"Nobody." He massaged my shoulders, making me relax, then chuckled softly. "As jealous as I got from people looking at you in the airport, I'm not about to let anyone see you now."

"I'm really stupidly pleased by that," I admitted, letting him undress me. In a few seconds, he had another dress pulled over my head, this one in a lighter weight fabric that fell to my ankles. "It must be time for a costume change. Can't wait to see what you're wearing."

He didn't answer my hint for information. Instead, he said, "Open your mouth just a little bit."

When I obeyed, I felt the touch of a lipstick on my lower lip, repairing the damage I'd done on the flight. This was so out of character for my husband. Yet it really wasn't. Henry had done shit like this all the time back in the day.

"You look so damned beautiful," he husked, kissing my forehead. "Ready to see your surprise?"

"Yes, Master." I couldn't wait, and accepted his arm around my waist as he led me through another door. We went outside, so maybe it was the same one we'd come in through.

"We're almost there. Just a few more yards."

He stopped and untied the blindfold and I blinked, my eyes adjusting to the bright mountain sunlight.

A modest white clapboard chapel painted with red roses stood in front of us. It had a drive through now, but the threadbare red carpet was the same, as was the recording of Vivaldi's Four Seasons emanating from cheap outdoor speakers.

"Oh, my God." I laid a hand over my mouth and tears pricked my eyes, spilling over to my cheeks.

"Ready to go in?" Henry asked, still wearing his jeans and white dress shirt. "I want to ask you something."

I nodded, unable to speak. My voice was stuck somewhere behind my thundering heart. He led me inside and turned me to face a large mirror. The white dress I wore was an almost exact duplicate of my wedding dress, but much sheerer. My nipples showed through, as did the rope harness around my hips and lady bits. The divided bodice split nearly to my waist, letting a peek of the inner curves of my breasts show. It was demure, but erotically sexy at the same time.

"Mr. and Mrs. Mercer, welcome!" a man said. I turned to face him and my knees nearly buckled at the sight of the celebrant who had married us all those years ago. He hadn't changed a bit, and still wore the Santa Claus beard and white suit.

I had no idea what to say. "Henry..." I swallowed and blinked when he dropped to his knees and held up a black velvet jewelry box about the size of a paperback book.

"It took almost losing you to make me realize what I had, baby girl. I might be the sadistic dom, but you hold all the power. Without you, I'm less than a man, and no dom at all."

He opened the box, revealing a platinum collar. Somewhat narrower than my steel training collar, it had a ring mounted in the center and channel-set diamonds along its length.

"Oh, my God." I held a hand to my lips,

swallowing the tears threatening to choke me.

"Natalie Kane, will you do me the honor of marrying me all over again?" Giving me a shamefaced grin, he winked. "I promise not to fuck it up this time."

Laughing helplessly, I went to my knees and threw my arms around his neck. His beard rasped against my face and I inhaled the familiar scent of his bay rum soap. "A thousand times, yes."

His eyes suspiciously wet, he helped me up and we followed the celebrant into the chapel.

Taking his position in front of us, the celebrant gave us a benevolent smile. "I remember marrying you two eighteen years ago. It is a great honor to be asked to renew your wedding vows. It's an even greater privilege to perform a collaring ceremony between a master and his cherished slave."

Laying a hand on my shoulder, he asked, "Natalie, will you kneel for your master and accept his collar?"

My heart swelling in my chest, I lowered myself to my knees.

EPILOGUE

Henry

I tipped my beer to my lips and took a small sip. I'd been nursing off the same bottle for over an hour. Kids still played chicken in the lake, enjoying the last few days of summer. I used to envy their careless joy, but not anymore.

Well, not really. I envied them the happiness coming their way. They would all meet that one person who made their lives complete. The one for whom they'd risk prison or worse, just for the chance to fall asleep next to them every night. That single moment of profound understanding. I wished for them the wisdom to keep it close and not throw it away like I almost had.

There was a lot less booze at this year's camping trip, and a lot more getting up at six in the morning to follow Ray on his morning run. Army strong, my ass. The man was a damned slave driver. I had to admit, whatever he'd done had stripped away the gut he used to carry around. He looked good. Even Logan followed us on Ray's impromptu death marches, and he was perfectly happy with his body the way it was.

I wasn't unhappy with mine, but chasing Natalie around the way she liked required a certain level of fitness, and she'd increased her workouts in response to me kidnapping her, which included kickboxing. A twinge of guilt pierced my chest. I'd scared the shit out of her, and she hadn't quite gotten over it.

My phone chimed with an incoming text from Natalie and I set my beer aside.

Natalie: *Safe in SFO. I'll send you the link for my speech in a few hours.*

Me: *Break a leg, baby girl. I love you.*

Natalie's business had gone utterly off the rails. And not in a bad way. She still created incredibly compelling art, and we traveled the world promoting her work and advocating for mental health in the kink community. That sixty/forty gap in our earnings went the other way these days. The best part was knowing she truly enjoyed her work. I just loved seeing her so happy.

Instead of finding another job, I'd taken over managing her marketing and scheduling. I was now her glorified personal assistant. The fringe benefits were amazing. Normally, I'd have gone with her to San Francisco, but she'd put her foot down and insisted I make my yearly camping trip.

"All right," Logan said, sitting in a camp chair across from me. "Spill the deets, dude. What happened with Natalie? She's like, all famous now, and I gotta know."

I took a pull from my bottle and tried to come up with some words, then grimaced when I realized everyone's attention was on me. "Well, I came home from our camping trip last year to a Dear John letter. I might or might not have kidnapped her after her debut show."

"Oh, fuck," Ray breathed. "That's why you wanted me to find her cell phone. God, you're an asshole. I could have gotten arrested."

Logan scowled, pinning me with a glare. "That is not cool, Henry."

I held up both hands. "Guilty as charged. It was

illegal and immoral as fuck, and I'm not proud of it, but I would have risked prison for a chance to get Natalie back."

"When you can all say you wouldn't do the same thing, let us know," Faris said quietly. "Until then, shut your fucking mouths and quit judging him."

Ray grunted, still giving me an evil glare. "Fine. I'd have locked Ally in a closet until she came around."

"Sorry," Logan muttered. "I shouldn't have leapt to conclusions."

"Why?" I asked. "You were right, and it wasn't one of my better ideas."

"It worked, didn't it?" Faris asked.

"Not helping," I muttered. "Kids, don't kidnap your wives. It won't end well."

"Enough," Ray announced, slapping his thighs. "It's time for our daily swim across the lake. We're all agreed that Henry was an idiot, so let's drop it."

Groaning, we all followed him into the water, but I didn't think any of us minded too much.

When we got back to our campsite, Ray sat next to me, his half-empty beer bottle dangling from lax fingertips. "So, kidnapping, eh?"

"Seemed like a good idea at the time," I replied, flushing at the memory. I'd nearly risked Ray with my shitall stupid plan.

"You're lucky you didn't get arrested."

I nodded, then said, "Well, I did get called in for questioning. My old boss accused me of assault."

Ray's eyes narrowed and he shook his head. "Not seeing it. Natalie would castrate you if you cheated on her. I'm assuming it got straightened out?"

I chuckled softly. Ray wasn't wrong, and the thought of having another woman made me sick. I was officially a one-slave master. I might whip her ass on a regular basis, but she had me whipped too. "Yeah. Just had to drop trou and show my dick to the detective."

"Shut up. I don't even want to know. I'm still trying to bleach my eyeballs from when you showed us your piercing." Scowling, he took another drink, then looked out over the lake. "So, it's all good now?"

"We're fantastic. Don't knock a Prince Albert until you try it. It makes Natalie crazy hot. How are things going with Ally?"

"Do tell," Faris said as he and Logan took seats on the other side of the campfire.

Instead of answering, Ray got up and tossed his empty in the bin we'd set aside for recycling. Returning to his seat, he leaned back and crossed his hands over his newly slimmed belly. "You're not the only idiot wandering in the woods," he muttered. "I went home and started jogging, and she thought I was getting in shape for another woman."

"Yeah, that's about as likely as me cheating on Natalie." I got up and fetched us both fresh drinks. "Did you get things settled with her?"

The corner of his mouth twitched up into an evil smile and he tipped his bottle at me. "You could say that, yeah."

⋅ ★ ⋅

I hope you enjoyed reading about Henry and Natalie. Please consider leaving a few words in a review. Love it or hate it, we want to know what you think!

Turn the page for a teaser from the next Dad Bod Dom novel by Maren Smith.

DAD BOD
DOMS
Ray

MAREN SMITH

Editor: Gabriella Wolek

Cover Design: Eris Adderly

Formatting: Cynthia Starrett

RAY

At ten minutes to the ungodly hour of five a.m., Ray Stewart's alarm went off. He bolted upright, smacking at the nightstand in an attempt to silence the shrill beeping before it woke his wife.

"Mm," Ally mumbled and rolled onto her stomach, pulling her pillow over her head. He could barely see more than just a shadow of her in the dark of the room. But what he could see didn't move again.

He waited breathlessly until from under those downy folds of cloth he finally heard the soft rumble of the snore his dainty five-foot-nothing wife would battle to the death before admitting she made. She was asleep. Thank God. What he was about to do would be hard enough. The last thing he wanted was a witness.

Especially if you can't hack it, said the treacherous half of his brain.

"I can fucking hack anything," he growled with that same military can-do that had gotten him through fifteen years in the army. Today, it got him out of bed two hours earlier than normal. Which was when he discovered that fifteen years of 'army tough' had nothing on a really cold floor.

Fuck! Whose bright idea was it to put tile instead of carpet in the bedroom? He glared at the lump that was his sleeping wife and quickly minced his way into the bathroom. From there his day only got worse.

Standing in front of the mirror, he brushed his

teeth, wet the bed-head out of his dark hair, and dejectedly eyed every one of those 'dad bod' pounds that had over the years quietly slipped onto what had once been a lean, mean, muscular machine of a soldier.

He flexed, completely appalled by the lack of definition in his reflection.

He used to be so buff. He was tall, too. Weren't taller people supposed to hide their extra pounds better than this?

He turned sideways, but that definitely didn't help. Where were all those well-defined bulges that used to ripple his arms, shoulders, chest and, well... everywhere? He struck a Herculean pose, but sadly his reflection didn't ripple. It jiggled. What the hell had happened?

A desk job, marriage to a wife who could cook like a dream, and three kids, that's what. He sucked in his stomach, felt a little ashamed of himself, and let it out again. It looked like he'd carried all three pregnancies. Turning sideways, he puffed his stomach out as far as it would go. Yup. Baby number four, right here. He had a dad bod, all right. Either that or he was eight months pregnant. Small wonder he and Ally weren't as hot between the sheets as they used to be.

Seeing this, thinking that, and knowing he had no one but himself to blame for falling this far out of shape didn't exactly motivate him. Rather, he got depressed. He did, however, finish brushing his teeth. At which point he could have just gone back to bed or wandered out to the kitchen in search of whatever was left of that quart of chocolate mint ice cream he'd bought two nights ago. Instead, he put on the brand-new jogging sweats he'd bought last night and his favorite sneakers, and just like he'd been telling himself since he got back from that revelation of a camping trip with the guys, he quietly let himself out of the house and went for a jog.

He hated running, despised every step of it. God knows, he'd gotten his fill of this particular torture back in his army days. He'd loathed it so much he'd refused to jog so much as one step right from the day he'd received his honorable discharge. So, it surprised him a little that he fell so seamlessly back into the rhythmic running cadence he used to dislike so much.

Yup, he still hated it, but that wasn't going to stop him from launching the first of what he was determined would become his new daily routine. Ten miles, just like in his military days.

Ten miles. No sweat. He could do this.

Except that ten miles turned into more like half a mile and instead of 'no sweat,' he was sweating all over. Panting, his hand clasped over the stitch in his side, Ray sucked for every gasp of air, but he kept going. Step after step, his run turned into more of a shuffle. He was the "jogging dead" and must have looked like it because two guys in a truck stopped to make sure he was okay.

"Yeah," he wheezed. "I'm fine."

Just taking my little pseudo eight-month gestation for a run. Ray tried to smile.

Judging by the look on the driver's face as he rolled the window back up again, he probably looked more like death about to keel over. But like any good Samaritan, at least he'd stopped and now, having done his good deed, they continued on to work.

Ray waved them off, his smile vanishing the second they were gone. God, his back. He stopped to stretch and check his watch to see how far he'd come. Not even three-quarters of a mile. Nine and a quarter left to go. He really was going to die.

You are not going to wuss out before you hit your first mile, he told himself angrily and started running again. Fifteen steps into it and already his confidence and determination were wavering. He wanted to quit. He wanted to quit so bad.

God must have been listening too and, as the old saying goes, He works in mysterious ways. Just as he was about to give in, from out behind a nearby house came one of the loudest and meanest cocker spaniels he'd ever met.

"Oh shit!" Ray took off as fast as his legs could pump him. He actually made three full miles before that little, furry, brown and white bastard stopped chasing him. He ran another block and a half to make sure the cocker spaniel wouldn't turn around and start chasing him again.

Slowing to a stop, he bent, hands on his knees, gasping to catch his breath.

That was when he met the German Shepherd.

***

Rolling out of bed at 6:30, Ally was a little surprised when she saw Ray's side was empty. Not just empty, the sheets were cold. She didn't know how long her husband had been up, but it must have been for a while. That in and of itself wasn't normal, but it wasn't terribly odd either. It wasn't common, but it wasn't unheard of for him not to sleep well if he was working a particularly stressful job. She honestly didn't know what he was working on right now; he hadn't talked about it, so Ally put it out of her mind. Mornings in the Stewart home with three kids six and under were a circus if she kept to her schedule and a shitshow if she fell behind. Right now, it was 6:32 on a Monday morning, and she was already two minutes behind.

Throwing on a robe, Ally hit the bathroom first. The hand towel she'd left folded on the sink last night was hanging neatly on the ring by the sink—a sure sign that Ray had been there. Taking care of herself, she then quickly bustled through the boys' room to wake Kevin, their oldest, and five-year-old Michael, and zipped into three-year-old Laylah's room to get her changed out of her night diaper into her morning pullups, before racing to the kitchen to get breakfast going.

Ray wasn't in the kitchen and the coffee maker hadn't been started. All right, now that was odd. That he wasn't still in bed catching those last few zzz's before his alarm went off at 6:45, okay. But that she didn't find him at the breakfast table, eating a piece of peanut butter on toast, working his way through his second cup of coffee and catching up on the news on his iPhone, now that was downright strange.

Breakfast immediately became cereal and milk so she could shave a few minutes off her schedule for a quick run through the house. He wasn't in his den, but his car was still in the garage. More alarming, however, was his cellphone, wallet and keys. The first two were sitting in the bowl on the table just inside the front door; the keys were not. Where the hell had he gone with his keys, but not his wallet, his phone, or his car?

Laylah let out a scream and Ally promptly headed back to the kitchen to squelch her sons' morning shenanigans before they could get out of hand.

The clock was a merciless taskmaster. She

couldn't throw a whole lot of attention into searching for Ray because she'd only allotted ten minutes for breakfast, and now she had faces to wash, and clothes to lay out, lunches to pack, homework to find, backpacks to make ready and, God, before she knew it, she was seven minutes late. Everyone was still in pajamas, and the school bus was due to be here in less than thirty.

And Ray was still nowhere to be seen. The garbage hadn't been taken out, he wasn't in the backyard or the basement, and every time she turned her back, the boys were sitting in front of the TV with their baby sister instead of getting their school clothes on.

"If you miss the bus twice in two weeks," she began in her best 'I have had enough' voice, but she never got to finish her threat. That was when the front door banged open and Ray stumbled in.

He was sweating, breathless and so red in the face that for a moment she honestly thought he might be having a heart attack. He was dirty too. The knee of his sweats was torn and a piece of broken ivy stuck out of the back of a hoodie she was pretty sure she hadn't seen before. It looked like he'd fallen and rolled in half the wilderness, which must have been some feat since they lived in the suburbs.

"Oh my God!" she declared, as he slammed the door and flattened himself against it. Venturing halfway down the short hallway between kitchen and him, she froze again. "What happened? Where have you been? Are you okay?"

"Cancel… our ADT," Ray wheezed between ragged gasps for breath. "Nobody's gonna… rob us. We've… too many… badass dogs in… oh my God, I'm dying… this neighborhood."

Glancing at the kids, all of whom were more engrossed in Sponge Bob than their potentially dying father, Ally ventured a few steps closer. Admittedly, if he was still cracking jokes, whatever was going on probably wasn't as dire as it appeared. "Where…" She quickly lowered her voice. "Where were you?"

"J… jogging." Grabbing the front of his hoodie, he fanned it in and out.

"Jogging?" she echoed, eyebrows arching. A sudden scream from the living room when the channel got changed averted her attention long enough for her to bellow, "I said go get dressed for school!" Just as fast as the boys stomped from the living room, she snapped her attention back to her husband. He was breathing easier now and his face wasn't quite as red, but instead of abating, that alarm that had stabbed through her gut when he'd come bursting in like this began growing roots. "But you hate jogging."

When he pushed off the door and stumbled past her, she trailed him down the other hall to their bedroom where he collapsed at the foot of the bed. Missing the mattress entirely, he sat on the floor.

The alarm inside her grew twice as many roots. "Are you all right?"

Letting his head fall back against the rumpled bedding, he huffed a soft, relieved laugh. "Yeah." He even offered a thumb's up for good measure.

She was not reassured. "Are you hurt?"

He looked down, seeming to take stock of himself. Plucking the ivy from his hoodie, he checked the hole in his knee. "Mostly just my pride."

"Mom!" their oldest wailed from down the hall. "I can't find Pickles!"

Half turning, she yelled back, "Stop looking for the cat and find your shoes!"

Problem dealt with, once more Ally considered her husband.

"I'll be fine," he panted, waving her off. And because she really didn't have time for this, she decided to let it go. Jogging? That was beyond odd, but sometimes people did weird things. Like, take up the one form of exercise they despised beyond all others. Out of the blue, and for no discernible reason.

The doctor said he needed to start watching his cholesterol, and had suggested diet and exercise. Maybe that's what Ray was trying to do. God knows he had a sedentary job and with three children, they didn't get out much. In fact, she couldn't remember the last time they'd gone out at all. Ray was a great provider, but he was absolutely a homebody.

Once upon a time she used to love the nightlife. The bars, the clubs, going out to dinners and movies and visiting with friends. The kids put a damper on that. These days, going out to dinner meant barbecuing on the patio, and visiting friends meant meeting the other moms at the kiddie park down the street. She wasn't complaining. She wouldn't give this up for the world. She loved her kids and her husband. She loved the life she had with them. Although admittedly, when she was twenty she never would have looked on all this and thought it would be her end-all be-all of perfect happiness. Yet it was. She really was happy.

He went jogging?

She seriously didn't have time to mess with this. The clock was ticking, and she was already running behind.

"You better get ready for work," she told him, and then hurried down the hall to make sure Michael was putting his shirt on right side out, find Kevin's shoes, and take the Legos out of Layla's mouth. She packed three lunches, two for the kids and one for her husband, and by the time he emerged dressed for work at the office, once more looking just like he did on any other day, the whole morning jogging routine could've been forgotten.

Except that it was hard to forget him coming in the door like that. In the back of her mind, Ally started ticking boxes. Ticking boxes was what she did best when she worried. He didn't have a doctor's appointment scheduled on the calendar that she knew of. He'd just had his physical, so that wasn't due. Maybe he'd just got on the scale this morning or one of the guys had said something over their weekend camping trip.

Maybe he'd met another woman.

That tiny kernel of dread that had been sending icy roots through the pit of her stomach instantly bloomed, becoming that much worse.

That was it, that had to be. There were only two reasons why a happily sedentary father of three, after eight years of marriage, would suddenly take up the one form of exercise he hated most. One, he was in dire health and she knew that wasn't true. She *knew* it. She'd seen the results of his last physical. In spite of carrying a few extra pounds and his cholesterol being on the high end of normal, he was in great shape. So that left only reason number two: he was trying to make himself look better for someone and that someone wasn't her.

Because she didn't care how he looked. Extra pounds or not, she loved him all the same. And really, how fancy did one have to be to spend family time sitting on the couch, eating a bowl of popcorn and watching Disney's *Little Mermaid* for the hundredth time.

"Don't be stupid," she told herself sternly, but in the back of her mind, her doubts were growing, settling all the way down in the pit of her stomach as he eventually came wandering out of the bedroom, freshly showered and dressed for the office. "Eggs and toast?" she asked.

"Celery," he replied.

Tick, went another box and the roots got that much colder.

He left for work and she wrangled the two boys onto the bus for school. Turning on Sesame Street for Laylah, she cleaned the kitchen, got laundry started, made the beds, picked up toys, sat at the foot of her bed for almost twenty minutes, and the whole time she couldn't even say what she thought about. Her head felt empty. There was just the cold, and the roots, and that tick in that box that she just kept turning over and over.

A man didn't start getting himself into shape so he could look his best on their beat-up living room sofa. Something else was going on—someone else— and Ally didn't have a clue what her name was.

What was she going to do? She had no idea.

Could she even blame him? She looked at herself, flushing shamefully as she drank in all the ways in which she'd let herself go. Her stomach that wasn't quite as flat as it used to be and her hips were way too round. No longer womanly; they were downright pudgy. Small wonder things had slowed down in the bedroom.

She wilted. She wasn't dressing her best for him these days, either. She was still in just her nightshirt and the robe she'd thrown on in case she had to go chasing down the street after one of the kids. Some days she never changed out of her pajamas at all, and just look at her feet! Her toenails hadn't seen a lick of nail polish since she last lost sight of them during her pregnancy with Michael. How long had it been since she'd worn makeup? Not since Laylah was born, she knew that much.

No, when it came to the romance department, she definitely wasn't putting in her fair share of effort. But that didn't mean she wanted him looking elsewhere and she sure didn't want him to leave. She loved him! She didn't care how much he weighed; his heart had always been bigger. That was one of the things she'd fallen most in love with all those years ago when first they'd met. He wasn't just big, he was strong. He made her feel protected, cared for. Cherished.

God. Folding over, elbows on her knees, she rubbed her face. What was she going to do? How could she fix this? Was it already too late?

No. Impossible. She refused to believe that. If it was too late, he'd be out the door already. For as long as he was still here, she had to have hope that somehow, someway, this—whatever or whoever *this* was—could be fixed. For as long as he was willing to lie beside her in their bed each night, she was going to work to correct what neglect and complacency had obviously damaged.

She had to put the spark back into her marriage.

But how?

Funny how, in that moment, her gaze accidently fell on that stack of old coffee table magazines that had been gathering like dust bunnies underneath her bedside table. Better Homes and Gardens, Good Housekeeping, Woman's Day... Cosmopolitan. She used to love reading those silly things and looking at the perfection reflected in all those family pictures.

These days, she barely had the energy to flip through a few pages before falling asleep at night, never mind trying to follow the advice. She didn't know why she kept buying them. She'd known for years that her home would never, ever come close to resembling anything out of Better Homes and Gardens. With three kids, household perfect was just plain unattainable. And yet, there had to be at least twenty or thirty magazines under that table, just waiting for her to find a few extra minutes in her tight schedule to throw them out.

Maybe it was a good thing she hadn't, a little voice in the back of her head whispered as she read one of the main headline article titles: *Ten Ways to Fall in Love Again*.

Well, that was appropriate.

She actually remembered buying this magazine, although not for that article. It was for the one above it done by some de-cluttering guru, who'd started her column by destroying whatever credibility she might otherwise have had with Ally when she'd advocated throwing out all her old books. *All of them*? Seriously, who the hell lived like that? Yeah, she could certainly do with a lot less clutter in her house and her life, but they could have her books when they pried them from her cold, dead fingers!

This other article, though.

Reaching for the magazine, she pulled it into her lap and, with Laylah in the living room, singing (and probably dancing) to something on Sesame Street, she flipped open to the corresponding page and read what it suggested.

"Remember what it was like when you first got together."

Ally started at that, and then she got cross. What good did *thinking* about anything do? She'd been thinking about it pretty much all morning, but that wasn't going to fix anything!

"Get in touch with your own sexuality."

That startled her even more. What, like masturbate? She almost threw the magazine back on the dust bunny stack where it belonged, but for the next suggestion on that thus-far useless list of ten.

"Make time for Date Night… with a surprise."

Ally stared at that for a long time. She could do that. That wouldn't be too difficult. When was the last time she and Ray had gone anywhere together, just the two of them? She could get a babysitter, put on some nice clothes, touch up her hair and face. She had no idea what she could do for the surprise part, but it had been forever since they'd gone anyplace nice. No kids allowed. Wine at dinner.

Of course, the way she was feeling, she might skip the wine altogether and go straight to martinis

Still, everyone had date nights these days, so why not them?

Closing the magazine, she tucked it back into the stack, hiding it below last month's edition of Good Housekeeping. All she had to do now, was make a few plans and figure out a surprise.

Preferably one that didn't include the kids tagging along on their very first date night because she couldn't find a last-minute babysitter.

ABOUT THE AUTHOR

Author of filthy smut, empty nester, and cat snuggler.

She's worked as a teacher, an actuary (her husband called her a bookie–which isn't too far from the truth), mother, scout leader, and is now enjoying semi-retirement writing the books she's always wanted to read.

Want to see what I'm up to next? Join my Raunchy Renegades at [http://www.facebook.com/groups/272762356598383/]. You can also sign up for my Newsletter [https://www.subscribepage.com/dad_bods]. As a bonus, everyone who signs up will recieve a FREE exclusive short story following up with Henry and Natalie.

Facebook - www.facebook.com/AuthorRaisaGreywood
Twitter - http://twitter.com/raisa_greywood
Instagram - http://instagram.com/raisagreywood

ALSO BY RAISA GREYWOOD

Bridgewater Brides
Their Wanted Bride

Cocky Hero Club
Sexy Scoundrel

Happily Never After (written with Sinistre Ange)
Demon Lust
Blood Lust

Holiday Daddies
Jennifer's Christmas Daddy
A Valentine for Chelsea

Shifter's Mates
The Tiger Queen
The Tiger King
The Leopard Mage
The Leopard Prince
The Jaguar Rogue
The Jaguar Knight

Standalone Titles & Anthologies
Longing and Lust & Other Short Stories
Bastard's New Baby
Ladder 54: Five Firefighter Romances
Masters of the Castle: Witness Protection Program
Dangerous Curves Ahead: An Anthology

Wicked Magic Trilogy
Wicked Deception
Wicked Truth
Wicked Fire